THREE MESSAGES AND A WARNING

THREE MESSAGES AND A WARNING

Contemporary Mexican Short Stories
of the Fantastic

Edited by **EDUARDO JIMÉNEZ MAYO**
and **CHRIS N. BROWN**

✳ ✳

✳

SMALL BEER PRESS
Easthampton, MA

Small Beer Press
150 Pleasant Street, #306
Easthampton, MA 01027
smallbeerpress.com
weightlessbooks.com
info@smallbeerpress.com

Distributed to the trade by Consortium.

Library of Congress Cataloging-in-Publication Data

Three messages and a warning : contemporary Mexican short stories of the
fantastic / edited by Eduardo Jiménez Mayo and Chris N. Brown. — 1st ed.
p. cm.
ISBN 978-1-931520-31-7 (trade pbk. : alk. paper) —
ISBN 978-1-931520-37-9 (ebook)
1. Fantasy fiction, Mexican. 2. Short stories, Mexican. I. Jiménez
Mayo, Eduardo, 1976- II. Brown, Chris N.
PQ7276.5.F35T47 2011
863'.087608972—dc23
2011016192

ISBN 978-1-931520-31-7 (paperback)
ISBN 978-1-931520-37-9 (ebook)

First edition 1 2 3 4 5 6 7 8 9

Printed on 50# Natures Natural 30% PCR recycled paper by
Cushing-Malloy, Inc. in Ann Arbor, Michigan.

Cover design by Jamie Stolarski (j-sto.conf).
Text design and composition by India Amos.

Text set in Espinosa Nova, which was designed by Cristóbal Henestrosa in 2010.
It is a revival of type used by Antonio de Espinosa, who was the foremost Mexican printer
of the sixteenth century and probably the first punchcutter on the American continent.

CONTENTS

�✍

The Return of Night

Three Messages and a Warning in the Same Email

The President without Organs

The Transformist

The Drop

Wolves

The Infamous Juan Manuel

INTRODUCTION

Better Than a Mirror

BRUCE STERLING

⚜

When one talks to Mexican science fiction writers, the subject of "Mexican national content" commonly comes up. Mexican science fiction writers all know what that is, or they claim to know, anyway. They commonly proclaim that their work needs more national flavor.

This book has got that. Plenty. The interesting part is that this "Mexican national content" bears so little resemblance to content that most Americans would consider "Mexican."

Americans, being the neighbors of Mexico, have a pretty fair idea of what Mexicans are up to. Some people would deny that, and claim that the norteamericanos only know the tourist-shop cliches, but that does Americans a disservice. Americans know about as much as any other non-Mexicans: they get it about Mexican food, Mexican music, the Fifth of May, hats and ponchos and serapes, snake and eagle flags, masked wrestlers, wealthy families, the oil business, seaside tourism, tequila, pulque and beer, cactus, jungles, fiestas, histrionic soap operas. . . .

Not only do Americans get it about that stuff, they admire those characteristics; they accept that as a kind of triumphant Mexican cultural imperialism, in a form of yanqui malinchismo. Americans can't do that stuff very well, so they know they ought to gracefully accept it.

But there's none of that in this story collection. Scarcely a trace of it, of that all-too-apparent kind of "Mexican-ness." Instead there are ghosts, mermaids, mutant fireflies, alien vampire bats . . . an obsession with buried treasure that leads a man straight to hell, an artist who vanishes into her own painting, an eerie plague of urbanized lions. . . .

That's what Mexican science fiction looks like when it's being most Mexican, and also most modern.

Mexican SF is intensely fantastic, but it's not very sci-fi. It's a New World science fiction without the stabilizing presence of American engineers and American gadget magazines. The structure of publishing in Mexico has always been Mexican; it lacks any middle-class. So there's a popular street level of wild-eyed fanzines, tabloids, and comic books, and an empyrean of Mexican fantastic literateurs who show an impressive awareness of Borges and Kafka. There's no middlebrow. Mexican SF is a science fiction with no popular mechanics, no problem-solving stories, and very little ideational extrapolation. "Hard SF" never took root in that soil.

Instead, this book offers what science fiction offers to Mexicans: a fantastic laboratory for identity issues. Most of these stories are brief, heartfelt, and low-key. They do not yowl from the rooftops at the multitudes; they have an epistolary, diaristic, or confessional air.

Melancholy ghosts abound, commonly treated with black humor.

There are no Mexican futuristic utopias on offer, but there are post-apocalyptic landscapes where Mexico itself becomes the ghost.

Artistic figures are everywhere in these stories, but they never claim any great fame or wealth; instead, they claim great secrets. The visionary maestro has blind eyes; the president has no organs. They seek dignity. Dignity and meaning, but dignity above all else.

Mexico and the USA have a somewhat fraught relationship, but we've always been there for one another, and by the standards of most nations our size, it's amazing how rarely we shoot each other. A European or Asian would have to conclude that we really do have a camaraderie, almost a sisterhood. It might not always feel that way on the ground, but the historical facts speak otherwise.

In today's conditions of rampant globalization, that kind of physical intimacy between nations takes on a different meaning. While the border between the nations grows taller and harsher, much abetted by the ill will of global guerrillas, the civil populations grow more intimate. Two literatures, based in different forms of paper, nurtured, sheltered, and neglected by their national presses and publishers, now see publishing in collapse—not just nationally, but most everywhere that ink ever hit paper.

The societies are radically changing, and, with them, the genres. It's about time to give the neighbors a second look. Things are not turning out the way the 20th century thought they would.

The United States of America is Mexicanizing much faster than Mexico is Americanizing. Ultra-wealthy moguls, class divisions, obsessions with weird religious cults, powerful factions who shun scientific fact, an abject reliance on fossil fuels and narcotics—these formerly Mexican characteristics have become USA all the way.

In conditions of globalization, you can always find new markets—or lose the ones you have—but you can never find old friends.

The face of an old friend can be better than a mirror, sometimes.

When Fixed Ideas Take Flight

EDUARDO JIMÉNEZ MAYO

༸

P︎ROBABLY NO other anthology of contemporary Mexican short stories has accomplished such a radical departure from the fixed adoration of literary mafias as the volume the readers have before them. This compilation of recent short stories of the fantastic includes some of Mexico's most established writers, spanning distinct generations; however, many of the authors appearing in it are considered emerging (in some cases marginal) voices on the Mexican literary scene. The editors have made a deliberate effort to uncover buried treasures of the fantastic from Mexico's Galilees and Galileans, places and persons relatively ignored by mainstream media in the Americas.

Regarding the genre of the fantastic, the editors have been careful to select pieces that cover the gamut of possibilities. Ghost stories, supernatural folktales, and extraterrestrial incursions into everyday life contrast with grounded scientific narrations of highly complex mental disorders and diseases that chronicle unusually heightened states of consciousness in which the borders of fantasy and reality reach unprecedented levels of ambiguity. Fixed stereotypes of Mexican identity are mobilized and transcended as the readers encounter the thoroughly cosmopolitan consciousness underlying these works.

The human fixation with disease, death and love constitutes a recurrent theme in this anthology. Jesús Ramírez Bermúdez's "The Last Witness to Creation," Horacio Sentíes Madrid's "The Transformist," and Ana Clavel's "Three Messages and a Warning in the Same Email" present cases of delusional individuals who either come to terms with their illness or succumb to it. Leo Mendoza's "The Pin" and Carmen Rioja's "The *Nahual* Offering" provide similar portraits of dementia, while generating waves of social critique: the former of the middle-class work ethic, the latter of exploitation of the indigenous poor.

René Roquet's "The Return of Night," Lucía Abdó's "Pachuca Second Street," Edmée Pardo's "1965," and Liliana V. Blum's "Pink Lemonade" form a quartet of death and resurrection of the apocalyptic variety. An earth devoid of life other than a lost colony of bats possessing obsessive ambitions to reproduce and thrive, the chaotic whirlpool of hyper-urban existence leading cataclysmically to physical and spiritual annihilation, the voluntary departure from the world of the living of two women who place their hopes in an extraterrestrial civilization, and a post-nuclear-holocaust planet in which men will kill for a glass of lemonade comprise the narrative repertory of this quartet.

María Isabel Aguirre's "Today, You Walk Along a Narrow Path," Iliana Estañol's "Waiting," Claudia Guillén's "The Drop," Yussel Dardón's "A Pile of Bland Desserts," Mónica Lavín's "Trompe-l'œil," Ana Gloria Álvarez Pedrajo's "The Mediator," "Óscar de la Borbolla's "Wittgenstein's Umbrella," and Guillermo Samperio's "Mr. Strogoff" constitute attempts at capturing human ambivalence in the face of death. Some may have reached the age when death would seem to be a phase of life's natural course, while the unexpected appearance of the undertaker may surprise others in the flower of their youth. Yet who among us, of any age, would not admit to spiritual perturbation when faced with the ultimate unknown: death, or, if one prefers, eternity? These stories comprise a myriad of ingenious yet vain attempts to assuage such perturbation through frantic imploration, physical comradery, home remedies, culinary enterprises, artistic representation, religious zealotry, philosophical exercises, and violent resistance.

Having arrived, finally, at the subject of love, we discover in Donají Olmedo's "The Stone," Hernán Lara Zavala's "Hunting Iguanas," Agustín Cadena's "Murillo Park," Beatriz Escalante's "Luck Has Its Limits," Queta Navagómez's "Rebellion," and Amélie Olaiz's "Amalgam" the most tender and cruelest manifestations of this emotion. Love's sublime power to transform our perception of reality arises in a truly mystical fashion in the first three stories, while the others emphasize the temporality or outright impossibility of mystical union in daily life. Personification, idealization, hallucination, prestidigitation, imagination, and recreation, respectively, become the literary resources that sustain the plots of these tales.

Although disease, death, and love form the cluster of themes most commonly encountered in these stories, we must not ignore the ultimate fixed idea of the genre of the fantastic as we know it today: that is, the fixation with the meaning and value of writing itself. Bruno Estañol's story, "The Infamous Juan Manuel," incarnates this theme in a most spectacular fashion. An aged treasure hunter opts for eternal condemnation over eternal peace upon learning that in hell he will be able to relive forever the contemplation of his belatedly discovered treasure. We would encourage a figurative reading of this story, if it were not for the fact that too many great writers and their works fall into oblivion.

True to the genre of the fantastic, the contemporary Mexican short stories in this anthology attempt the impossible—capturing the extraordinary moment when humanity's fixed ideas on disease, death, and love inexplicably loosen and take flight thanks to the regenerative power of the literary imagination.

Introduction

CHRIS N. BROWN

During a recent vacation to the Mexican coast, I acquired an unusual souvenir: a hand-painted votive plate featuring the Virgin of Guadalupe fighting Osama bin Laden to prevent him from detonating any nuclear weapons in the Americas. In the plate, Osama is a much bigger figure than la Virgen, who is herself just a little bit larger than the devil over Osama's shoulder. When I asked the shopkeeper, an expat Italian woman typical of the sandalista-occupied Mayan town of Tulum, where she had found the piece, she explained that "it was made by ancient peoples."

The stories in this anthology were not made by ancient peoples. They were made by 21st century people. But they share with my virginal Osama plate a confounding of our expectations of what Mexican artistic self-expression is supposed to look like. While our cover features some skeletons with monarch butterfly wings, you will not find any Day of the Dead tropes in these stories, or any images from the Frida Kahlo calendar. You may find some things that you are inclined to categorize as magic realism, but you will be hard-pressed to situate them in some humid post-colonial cultural haze.

This anthology endeavors to collect stories that express a 21st century perspective, of a multicultural, media-drunk, post-postmodern society. Stories that participate in a panoply of cross-cultural conversations, while doing so in a uniquely Mexican voice that runs through the stories, even though the authors may come from very different ends of the Mexican literary scene. This is a literary culture that still enjoys mass appreciation of the importance of verse, where large crowds gather in public plazas to hear poets read their work. But it is also a culture whose everyday consciousness includes, alongside folkloric traditions and indigenous cuisines integrated into the fabric of daily life, memories of seeing a space probe's photos of the surface of Mars, and minds plugged into the mediated networks that dominate our global perceptions.

The stories come from a culture that itself would probably never collect these authors in a single volume. Perhaps reflecting the diverse interests of the editors—a scholar of Spanish literature and a science fiction writer who independently approached the same publisher with a very similar idea (and who, oddly, both also happen to be lawyers), this anthology includes established figures of the literary mainstream alongside products of the indigenous Mexican science fiction scene. While the regard for the likes of Phillip K. Dick and J.G. Ballard espoused by writers such as Roberto Bolaño has given more credibility to sf as a literature of worth among Mexican culturati, Mexican writers who declare themselves authors of *ciencia ficción* often feel like outsiders, no more welcome at the party than a pulp space squid at a reunion of Raymond Carver characters. But grouped together here, one can see a common perspective that reveals the pieces as flowing in the same river.

These are all stories in which rational explanations for remarkable things are not required or expected. Products of a world that the authors all understand cannot really be explained with numbers and laws, a world full of phenomena for which the priests, policemen, and psychics have no credible answers. Perhaps these authors recognize that some things are better left without explanations, just as they realize that some stories do better without too much "story" structure —products of a literary culture in which paragraph-long atmospheres count, and in which catholic rules of time and tense, point of view, and the separation between reality and fantasy can be broken without sanction or permanent banishment to generic ghettos. These are stories that can walk through walls. Even border walls.

The stories, and their authors and editors, also owe a great debt to the translators who have undertaken the difficult task of bringing these works of a uniquely Mexican Spanish into a form we hope preserves them largely intact for English language readers to fully experience their magic. Our translators are all volunteers, some of them young American scholars of Spanish literature, some American writers with an adequate dose of Spanish language competency and a strong desire to decode the work of another, and in some cases Mexican or expat friends and neighbors of the authors. This was not an easy book to collect and compile, but we hope you agree the effort has produced fantastic results.

THREE MESSAGES AND A WARNING

Today, You Walk Along a Narrow Path

MARÍA ISABEL AGUIRRE

Translated by REBECCA HUERTA

For my father, Emilio F. Aguirre Astudillo

ॐ

What will you be when you are in the night
and at the end of the road?

—FERNANDO PESSOA (ÁLVARO DE CAMPOS), *Odes*

YOU WALK ALONG a narrow, earthen path. In the distance you see the hills and cornfields. You have the impression of having been walking for quite a while. It must be six or seven in the afternoon, since the light is already very scarce. It is just the moment in which darkness will fall, but it is still day. In the distance, you perceive the festivities and uproar from the community of Huitzuco. It is the celebration of the Solemnity of All Saints. Many candles can be seen through the hustle and bustle. You perceive the smell of the food being served. They are dishes that you have not savored in years.

Suddenly, beside you, walks another person. You observe him for an instant and detect very familiar features in him. He is your uncle. You know this because you saw him once at the home of your grandparents; although, this is the first time you will be able to speak to him up close. He turns toward you. Until that moment, he seemed not to have noticed your presence. He looks at you with strangeness. Perhaps he does not recognize you for sure, but he seems to guess who you are, and he greets you:

"Hey . . . what are *you* doing here?"

"I came to participate in the festivities, and you?"

"Same here; this is when the town is happiest. It's been years since I've seen it like this . . ."

"How long have you been coming back here to celebrate?"

"Coming back? About twenty years, I guess; and you?"

"It's my first time . . . I was feeling a bit lonely out there . . ."

"Oh, don't worry; we all feel bad after a while and long to come back here. You'll get used to it."

Your uncle falls silent and you follow his lead. You stop together at a place where the path ends. In the distance, you catch sight of some lights: some yellow paper lanterns have just been lit.

"Well, nephew, they are waiting for me. Stay here if you want; honestly, I won't be long."

"All right uncle," you answer.

You see him move deep into the darkness and disappear into it. Time passes and he has yet to return. Moved by curiosity, you want to follow him down the path where you saw him disappear, but at that very moment someone behind you pronounces your name. You turn around and discover your Aunt Enedina.

"Good evening, aunt, I'm so happy you've come!"

"My dear nephew, who are you waiting for?"

"Uncle Juan. He told me he wouldn't be long in coming back."

"We buried Juan years ago. He was killed because he stole some cattle and slept with another man's wife."

"But I just spoke with him a little while ago; he was happy to be back in town."

"You should come with me. This is a bad place to wait. There are many lost souls wandering about. Let's go eat with the others."

"Aunt Enedina . . . where are you?"

You continue walking along the narrow path. The turmoil of the crowds and the movement of the lanterns come into view, yet they appear to be disconnected. Finally, you realize that each light corresponds to an individual person.

You are there, looking for someone familiar. Suddenly, you see a light that is more intense than the others; a deep and profound one. You move closer. You discern among the shadows a few familiar faces: your Uncle Nicolás and Aunt Adela. They tell you that they have come from afar to greet you.

Suddenly, you see your father. It cannot be. You never have believed in such things. What things? Your little daughter Elvirita is there too . . . it's impossible. Isn't it? You know that it is, but you want to believe it is true because you can see her! She is standing right there in front of you. You run toward them, you want to embrace them, you want to talk with them; but you can't. They take no notice of you, or perhaps they don't want to see or hear you.

They have left only some offerings at the foot of your tomb, some fruit and a lit candle.

The Guest

AMPARO DÁVILA

Translated by ANNA GUERCIO

૭৯

I'LL NEVER FORGET the day he
came to live with us. My husband brought him back from a trip.

By then we'd been married three years, had two children, and
I wasn't happy. To me, my husband was like a piece of furniture
that you're used to seeing in a certain spot, but which no longer
makes the slightest impression. We lived in a small town, far
from the city and hard to get to. A half-dead town on the verge
of disappearing.

I couldn't stifle a shriek of horror the first time I saw him.
He was dismal, sinister. With huge yellow eyes, unblinking

and almost round, that seemed to cut straight through people and things.

My wretched life became hell. The very night he arrived I begged my husband to spare me the torture of his presence. I couldn't help it; I was filled with horror and distrust. "He's completely harmless," said my husband, looking at me with marked indifference. "You'll get used to having him around, and if you don't . . ." There was no way to convince my husband to take him away. He stayed in our home.

I wasn't the only one who suffered. Everyone in the house— my children, the woman who helped me with chores, her little boy—we were all terrified of him. Only my husband enjoyed having him there.

From day one, my husband gave him a corner room. It was a big space, but damp and dark. That's why I never went in there. He, however, seemed pleased with the room. As it was rather dark, he adapted by necessity. He'd sleep 'til nightfall, and I never did figure out when he went to bed.

I lost what little peace I'd enjoyed in my big house. During the day, everything was ostensibly normal. I'd always get up very early, dress the kids, who were already awake, feed them breakfast, and keep them occupied while Guadalupe straightened the house and went out to run errands.

The house was quite large, with a garden in the middle and rooms arrayed around it. Between the rooms and gardens, we had corridors to buffer the bedrooms from the frequent onslaughts of rain and wind. To keep such a big house orderly and the garden impeccable—my daily morning task—was hard work. But I loved my garden. The corridors were filled with vines that bloomed practically year-round. I remember how much I loved to spend my afternoons in those corridors, seated between the perfume of the honeysuckle and the bougainvillea while I sewed clothes for the children.

In the garden we grew chrysanthemums, pansies, Alpine violets, begonias, and heliotrope. While I watered the plants, the children amused themselves searching for worms among the leaves. Sometimes they'd spend hours, silent and focused, trying to collect the drops of water that dripped from the ancient hose. I couldn't help stealing occasional glances at that corner room. Even though he spent all day sleeping, I could never be too sure. Lots of times I'd be making dinner and suddenly his shadow would fall across the wood stove. I'd feel him behind me . . . I'd drop whatever was in my hands and run from the kitchen screaming like a madwoman. He'd return once more to his room as if nothing had happened.

I think he ignored Guadalupe completely, never harassing or even going near her.

Not so with my children and me. He hated them and was always lying in wait for me. Every time he came out of his room, I was thrown into the worst nightmare anyone can know. He'd set himself up at a little table across from my bedroom door. I stopped leaving. Sometimes, thinking he was asleep, I'd sneak toward the kitchen to prepare a snack for the children, and I'd stumble on him in some dark corner of the corridor, hiding beneath the vines. "I'll be right there, Guadalupe!" I'd scream desperately.

Guadalupe and I never discussed him by name; it seemed like doing so would mean relinquishing our reality to that dark being. We'd always say, "There he is, he's gone out, he's sleeping, he, he, he . . ." He only ate twice a day, once when he rose at dusk and again, sometimes, in the early morning before going to sleep. Guadalupe was responsible for bringing him his food; I can say with certainty that, inside that room, the poor woman felt the same terror as I. Meat was all he'd eat—he wouldn't even touch other food.

When the children went to sleep, Guadalupe would bring my dinner to our room. I couldn't leave them alone, knowing that he might be up. As soon as she'd finished her chores, Guadalupe and her little one would retire to their room and leave me alone, watching my children sleep. Since the door to my room was always left open, I could never sleep, fearing that at any moment he might come in and attack us. Closing the door wasn't even an option; my husband always got home late and if he'd found it closed he'd have thought . . . And I mean he got home really late. You work such long hours, I remarked once. I wonder if work's the only thing keeping you out . . .

One night, I was woken at nearly two in the morning, hearing him in the distance . . .

When I woke, I saw him at my bedside, looking at me with his fixed, penetrating stare . . .

I jumped up and hurled the gas lamp I kept lit at night. Our little town didn't have electricity and I couldn't stand the dark, knowing that at any moment . . . he deflected the lamp and slipped away as it crashed on the brick floor with the gasoline bursting into flames. If Guadalupe hadn't heard my screams, the whole house would have burned down. My husband had neither time to listen to me nor any concern for what went on in our house. We spoke only when necessary. Over time, our affection and our words had run dry.

I still feel sick when I think about this . . . Guadalupe had gone shopping and left little Martín asleep in the crib where he rested during the day. I went to check on him intermittently; he was sound asleep. It was around noon. I was combing my children's hair when I heard the little boy's howl mixed with strange grunts. When I reached the bedroom I found him cruelly hitting the child. I don't know what happened, but I somehow got hold of the boy and managed to swing a club I found in my hand, attacking him with all the rage that had been building for so long. I don't know if it did much damage, since I passed out cold. When Guadalupe got back from her errands, she found me distraught and her little one bleeding and covered in bruises. She was overcome by pain and fearsome fury. Fortunately, the boy survived and healed quickly.

I was scared that Guadalupe would go away and leave me all alone. If she didn't, it was because she was a noble, valiant woman who had deep affection for me and my children. But that day saw the birth of a hatred in her, one that demanded vengeance.

When I told my husband what had happened, I begged him to take him away, pleading that he might kill our children like he tried to kill little Martín. "You get more hysterical every day. It's really painful and depressing to see you like this . . . I've told you a thousand times that he's harmless."

I thought then that I should flee from that house, from my husband, from him . . . But I didn't have any money and getting in touch with the outside world was almost impossible. Without friends or relatives to turn to, I felt as lonely as an orphan.

My children were terrorized; they didn't want to play in the garden and wouldn't leave my side. Whenever Guadalupe went out to the market, we'd shut ourselves up in my room.

"This situation cannot continue," I told Guadalupe one day.

"We have to do something, and soon," she replied.

"But what can we two do alone?" Alone, true, but full of such hate . . .

Her eyes gleamed strangely. I was terrified and thrilled.

Our chance came when we least expected it. My husband went to the city on business. He'd be back, he told me, in twenty days or so.

I don't know if he realized that my husband had left, but that day he woke up earlier than usual and stationed himself in front of my room. Guadalupe and her son slept in my room that night, and, for the first time, I was able to shut the door.

Guadalupe and I spent almost all night scheming. The children slept quietly. Every so often, we heard him walk up to the bedroom door and bang on it furiously . . .

Guadalupe sawed several planks of wood, big, strong ones, while I looked for a knife and some nails. When everything was ready, we tiptoed over to the corner room. The sliding doors were ajar. Holding our breath, we turned the bolts, locked the doors with a key, and used the hammer and nails to seal up the room completely. While we worked, big drops of sweat rolled down our faces. He didn't make a sound, seemingly fast asleep. When everything was finished, Guadalupe and I held one another and wept.

The days that followed were frightful. He survived a long time without air, light, food . . . At the beginning, he pounded on the door, threw himself against it, yelling desperately, clawing the wood . . . Neither Guadalupe nor I could eat or sleep, the screams were so terrible! Sometimes we were scared my husband would return before he was dead. If he were to find him like this . . . ! He resisted mightily, I think he made it nearly two weeks . . . Then, one day, we didn't hear anything.

Not even a cry . . . We waited two days more, however, before opening the room.

When my husband returned, we greeted him with the news of his sudden and disconcerting death.

Murillo Park

AGUSTÍN CADENA

Translated by C.M. MAYO

✺

Monday to Friday, past two in the afternoon, at one of the shaded benches in Murillo Park, there was an appointment no one had made formally. Its witnesses were the poplars and jacarandas that are still there offering their freshness.

The office allowed me two hours for lunch, from two until four. That was a lot of time for a forty-year-old bachelor used to eating quickly and alone. So it was that, having finished up at a nearby lunch counter, there wasn't anything else to do but kill time by walking the streets and looking at the shops; although in this once elegant but now down-on-its-luck neighborhood, there wasn't much to see. The houses looked rickety, like those women who were lovely in their younger days and decades later preserved only the scent of wilted flowers. That's how the houses were there: tall, shady, silent, painted in a scabby color under the smothering ivy with double-sloping roofs and the shutters always closed. On the main avenue there weren't many shops. After a few visits I knew everything they had to sell. There was only a watchmaker's shop, some shoe stores, a bridal boutique, and a small passageway full of coin dealers and herbalists. But there were many government offices.

I don't like parks. They resemble refuges for bums, people looking for work in the newspapers, exhibitionist couples; worst of all at midday, when they fill with teenagers away from school on their lunch hour. But that day—the first day—I gave in. I gave in because of the heat—it was thirty-eight degrees Celsius—and because there was nothing else to do, and because I'd had a bad day. In the morning, before leaving my house, I'd had an argument with my sister over some stupidity. We were two singletons whose characters had been embittered by bachelorhood and spinsterhood and a lack of dreams. Then, in the office, I had to redo a job because of my boss, a girl just out of university and full of herself. So that's how it happened that I went to Murillo Park, found a shady bench, and sat down.

It was fortunate that there weren't many people: a couple in their forties, pale and about one and a half meters tall, though maybe the woman was a little bit taller; a man of about thirty, olive-skinned, with an enormous gold bracelet on his wrist; an older woman, and, on the same bench as her but at its opposite end, a handsome young man wearing a cheap and badly cut suit. Strangely, they were all asleep. It was because of the heat, I assumed. Without realizing it, I also fell asleep.

I was in a good mood the rest of the afternoon and, trying to come up with an explanation, I told myself it had been many years since I'd slept so peacefully as I had for that spell in Murillo Park. It shouldn't be surprising that I returned the next day. Yes, I returned the next day and the next and then every day, from Monday to Friday. The siesta under the trees became my daily and obligatory portion of earthly pleasure. In time I came to have my own bench, almost my own, one that everyone recognized was for me, and they respected that; a bench that waited for me every afternoon at the same hour, like a faithful girlfriend. Of course, on occasions I had to share it with strangers to me and my fellow sleepers. Once I even had to listen to a lovers' quarrel barely thirty centimeters from my right ear.

We came to know each other. We didn't converse much, as we went there to nap, but we managed to learn a few things: each others' names, where we worked. For example, Martínez, the guy with the gold bracelet, preferred to sleep in the park rather than his office because he snored and farted at the same time. And nobody gave him a hard time; nobody felt the need to wear a mask. The couple of near-dwarves had lost hope of having a child after who knows how many tests and treatments. They worked in the same building, though not in the same office, and they liked to watch the kids coming out of the high school. They went there, sat on their bench and closed their eyes to engender in their minds their impossible offspring. Martínez was fed up with his wife: he did everything he could to avoid her, but he wouldn't think of divorce. On Fridays, instead of taking his siesta, he would visit a young and attractive woman who accepted money from him. As for the young man, Ramiro, he had fallen in love with one of his co-workers in the ministry. He asked our advice about how to dress, which cologne to use, where to take her, and what gifts to give her.

This is how I met Jorge, the older lady I had seen that first afternoon. Jorge was her last name, not her first, but that is what she liked to be called. She was a widow, still comely, with a voice that betrayed her vice of smoking while possessing velvety nuances enhancing its femininity. She dressed elegantly and had a large bosom, with stretch marks, which glistened in the sun thanks to her décolletage.

"I'm much obliged," she said distantly, as if with nostalgia, the first time we spoke, when, nodding on the bench, she had dropped her magazine and I had bent down to retrieve it. It was printed in sepia. I couldn't help but see the title, *Mexico Today*. I had never seen that one in the kiosks.

"It's nothing," I said modestly, and before she had a chance to nod off, I took my chance to start a conversation:

"I've seen you around here. Do you work nearby?"

She fanned herself a little with the magazine and smiled.

"I work in the Montecarlo. Do you know it?"

"The Montecarlo?" It seemed to me I'd heard that name somewhere, but I couldn't place it.

"Don't tell me you haven't heard of it!"

"Well . . ."

"I'm in charge of the coat check and other small things. I start at six in the afternoon."

"Ah," was the only thing I could think of to say. I was quiet for a moment, looking ahead, where two high school girls were teasing each other with a kind of slang that, in my time, only men would use. I was embarrassed that Jorge, so ladylike, should hear this. But Jorge wasn't hearing anything now: she was snoring. She slept with her mouth open and nearly falling over onto my shoulder. Her magazine had once again fallen from her hands and was coming apart in the puddle under the bench.

All that afternoon and even into the night, once in bed, I thought about this woman and asked myself, where did she work? Why was she dressed and made up like that? What were the magazines she was reading about? What was her life like? There was something about her that intrigued and attracted me very much. It seemed to me that I had dreamt about her once, when I was a boy or a teenager: a dream with the scent of orange trees in blossom.

The next day we met again. I couldn't wait to ask her the questions on the tip of my tongue:

"Tell me about yourself, Jorge. Tell me about your life."

"I have made many mistakes," she answered in a conclusive tone, and she closed her eyes without saying more. I didn't know when exactly she fell asleep, there on the bench, breathing deeply through her red-painted lips.

The next day I did not see her. But I sat next to Martínez and I asked him about her.

"I haven't noticed her," he said. "What does she look like?"

I described her for him, but it was useless.

"No, well, the truth is, I don't remember her."

After that came a long Saturday without news of Jorge nor any way to talk with her. "Had I made her mad?" I asked myself several times. My sister noticed and she asked me what was wrong. I told her the whole story.

"What kind of crazy person have you found? The Montecarlo was a nightclub back in the forties."

"It must be a different one," I said, mentally erasing the

possibility that there was something strange about Jorge, "a new one with the same name."

"And then her name, Jorge . . . don't you suspect she might be a lesbian, Ducky?"

"I already told you, that's her last name." In the first place, I was annoyed by her manner of talking to me. In the second, I hated being called that ridiculous nickname, which my mother had given me when I was a kid.

"All right, then . . . no need to get upset."

We were quiet for a long time. We'd just eaten, and, though it was turned on in front of us, the television had lost our attention.

Like every Saturday, my sister and I rested for a while after lunch and then we got ready to go to the neighborhood movie theater. There I relaxed, I stopped thinking about silly things, and I enjoyed the picture. Then we went for donuts and hot chocolate, another thing we did every Saturday. Finally we went home in peace, and there, in peace, I would fall asleep but never dream. Sunday went by quickly: that was the day we cleaned the house.

The following Monday, at last, I saw Jorge. Trying to act disinterested, I asked her what she'd done on Saturday.

"I went to the movies with my sister," she said with satisfaction.

Now we're getting somewhere, I thought: she has a sister and she likes the movies. Just like me.

"What a coincidence: I also went to the movies with my sister. Maybe we were in the same room, at the same time, without realizing it."

"I went to the opening night of *A Different Dawn*. And you?"

"Um . . . we went to see *The Terminator*. That's what they were showing at the theater near my house."

"Ah," Jorge answered, distractedly. "I haven't heard of that one."

"And the one you went to see, did it have anyone famous in it?"

"Of course! It had Julio Bracho. And it starred Andrea Palma and Pedro Armendáriz."

It sounded to me like one of the pictures from the forties they showed on Channel 4, but I didn't say anything. Jorge didn't seem to want to talk. She fell asleep right away.

That night, my sister asked what had happened with her. I didn't tell her everything; I left out the part about the movie. I didn't want her to annoy me again, and she didn't.

Jorge and I continued to see each other on that bench. Days went by, weeks. There was a moment when I tried to get more out of her. She preferred to hide, to turn my questions around on me. I answered, recounting my life without secrets. What did I have that was worth hiding? We became friends, more than friends. That is, we grew very close, very much alike in some sense—we both liked peanut candies with caramel and the candied figs the street vendor would take from bench to bench—but we never managed to have what one would call a romance. We never even saw each other away from those benches. On the verge of suspecting Jorge might be crazy, I repressed the thought. It was that every month she brought a new issue of *Mexico Today*. And every time I asked if I could see it, I saw that it was fifty years old and advertised things that were no longer available: Ipana toothpaste, The Business and Banking School on Palma 27, *Printemps de Paris* perfume, Boujois red lipstick that purportedly "avoided the painted look," Quina Laroche tonic wine, Eno fruit salt, and who knows how many other equally strange things.

Maybe there could have been something more between us, but I didn't want it. I was afraid. I was afraid because I had dreamt about her when I was little and I didn't want to ruin this dream. One afternoon, taking advantage of the fact that everyone in the park was asleep and there was no one to see us, I took Jorge's hands in mine. She looked at me intensely, her eyes very bright under the painted blue shadow of her eyelids, and she said to me:

"Next week maestro Lara will play at the Montecarlo. Why don't you go? I can get you one of the best seats, and look, if you're not too sleepy to stay up late and you want to wait for me, afterward we could go out somewhere. The Smyrna closes later."

"Maestro Lara . . ." Was she talking about Agustín Lara? That was too much. And nonetheless, it didn't matter. Truly, it didn't matter. I was able to keep holding her gaze, but not her hands. I was about to tell her, "I'm afraid our friendship is doomed not to last," but I sensed that she wouldn't understand me. Her hands now free, she put one on my thigh and winked at me.

"Come on, you'll see, you won't regret it."

Although my heart started to beat fast, there was something in this gesture that seemed repulsive to me. I repressed it, relegating it to the depths of my consciousness. It didn't fit with the woman I had dreamed about as a boy: a woman still young, subtle, and beautiful, despite the dream being now very old.

"Instead, Jorge, why don't you come have tea with us? My sister makes fritters."

"I'll telephone you soon," she said dryly. But she didn't call. She didn't call, and, furthermore, she stopped coming to the park. "What if I upset her?" I asked myself. Maybe I said something I shouldn't have. Or maybe she thought me very silly. Why didn't I take advantage of the opportunity she was giving me? Anyone else in my place would have known what to do, I reproached myself continually. Every afternoon in Murillo Park I hoped to see her, and at night I had elaborate fantasies of scenes in which Jorge and I found each other again in her world, not this so imperfect world. I saw her dressed in a vaporous organdy dress with very high heels, seated on a black velvet cushion, smoking. We enjoyed ourselves until midnight in exciting places, after which we would begin to kiss in the streets, leaning against antique automobiles slick with the night's dew; drunk and happy, we would lurch out into the fog to walk down a street with no end.

I asked Martínez about her again. I asked all the others. They not only had not seen her, they said they didn't know her. They're making fun of me, I thought. How could it be possible that not one of them had noticed her? She with whom I had shared my siesta on so many afternoons! No, they insisted, they didn't know her, they hadn't seen me talking to anyone on that bench; they didn't remember any woman of that description.

I began to spend the period of my siesta looking for Jorge. I found the Yellow Pages for recent years, and there I looked for the Montecarlo. There were four motels that rented rooms by the hour and some public baths under that name, all in different parts of the city. The time I had for my siesta wasn't enough; I had to invest more and more hours into investigating her whereabouts. I, who always took refuge at home at twilight, got to know the city at night. I got to know horrible places, none with an employee named Jorge handling the coat check: they didn't even have a coat check. Finally, I confirmed the address of the old Montecarlo. There wasn't anything there anymore. Nothing! I regretted being so stupid. Out of nothing but shyness I had never asked Jorge for her telephone number, though she had mine. She never called me, however, and I never found her: and after some months, I returned to my routine of siestas in Murillo Park and quit fantasizing. I went back to my friends: Martínez, the couple, young Ramiro.

For seven years, these people and I met from Monday to Friday in Murillo Park, sleeping thirty minutes on each occasion. Therefore we must have shared some 1,800 hours of sleep: 75 days! Sleep is the most intimate of all acts, the one that requires the most trust in others. A sleeping human is a vulnerable creature who has voluntarily abandoned himself to the mercy of others. Young Ramiro was the first to desert; he found a better job, in another part of the city. The couple retired, yet for a while they kept coming to take their siesta with us out of habit. Eventually, they stopped coming altogether. Others took their place: an ex-alcoholic or "dry drunk," as he called himself, a neighborhood vendor who suffered from gout, a divorced woman full of resentment.

I never discovered anything more about Jorge. Then one day, as I interpret the event, she said farewell to me. Here's what happened: feeling that I was too old to be a novice in matters of women, and since I couldn't find anyone to keep me company, I overcame my embarrassment and called a house of prostitution that advertised in the newspaper. I asked if among the girls there might be one of around fifty years. They told me no, that all were less than twenty-four, but that they could give me the telephone number of another house where I would find what I was looking for. I wrote down the number. It took me two weeks to bring myself to call, and finally I made an appointment, a gratuitous act, and took a taxi to the establishment. Embarrassed that the driver would know where I was going, it wasn't easy for me to give him the address.

It turned out to be a run-down place. There was a rose-colored parlor with a sofa covered in plastic where one sat down to see the women presented one at a time. As they came down, I looked around the place, trying to keep calm. I noticed that in the back there was a large radio in a console on top of which there was a photograph of Pedro Infante in a wooden picture frame, chipped at the edges. I told myself, "There's something of her here." And when the girls had all come down, I felt happy. They were all mature; the youngest must have been over forty. Suddenly, I wasn't nervous anymore; I just felt anxious to choose. The woman who led me upstairs to her room looked like Jorge. The likeness was very close, but it wasn't her. She possessed neither her skin, warmed by the two o'clock sun, nor her perfume, nor her velvety voice. I paid a lot, and I tried to get the most out of it.

When I came down the stairs on my way out the women had turned on the radio. I noticed that it was tuned to XEW, "The Intimate Hour with Agustín Lara." Just then a woman whose voice was the same as Jorge's called the station and said:

"I want to request the song *Impossible*, dedicated to Ducky, from a friend."

She didn't have to say her name. I knew it was she, and I even forgave her the "Ducky," although I couldn't help wondering how she knew about my ridiculous nickname.

Her message gave me back my peace of mind. I knew that there was no such program on XEW, nor any other station. I knew that Agustín Lara had died in 1970 and that the Monte-carlo, the Smyrna Club, and all those places ceased to exist a long time ago; but sometimes, all of a sudden, as I passed by one of those businesses that still had an old radio, "The Intimate Hour with Agustín Lara" would come on and almost without static. I would stop for a few minutes to hear the people calling in asking for dedicated songs. When I hear that velvety voice that calls me "Ducky" I close my eyes and once again breathe in the freshness of the poplars and the jacarandas while I hold Jorge's age-spotted, nicotine-stained hands in mine.

The Hour of the Fireflies

KAREN CHACEK

Translated by MICHAEL J. DELUCA

ৎ৯

LEAVING OPEN THE apartment door is part of the plan. I run into my landlord on the stairway. Today he sounds like a walking rattle; he carries a bottle of tablets in each coat pocket. "Vitamin supplements," he says. "When you're twice your age, you'll understand." I wink my thanks at him for his dictum. I don't tell him that's not part of the plan. Nor do I mention how the company I work for has disappeared from the circuit in less time than it takes to light a lamp, without paying me a cent. I smile my usual good-bye and look down the stairs. He grabs my arm and, with a paternal air, warns me not to stay out too late: the hour of the fireflies is about to begin.

Mama doubled over laughing when she heard my plan: she said it was crazy. But so is falling prey to the collective inertia. To transcend like a portable media player, I think it's just as obscene as going to dance at this new place: "the Laboratory." My grandparents spent twenty-seven months locked in a laboratory. The majority of the captives died, electrocuted, driven insane, the victims of prolonged exposure to artificial light. But what the hell! Let's dance—who can feel bad about something everyone thinks never happened? So what if my fingernails shine at night?

When I was a kid I used to believe if I changed my name I could leave behind everything I knew: the stories I'd heard at family meals, the memory of the image files my grandpa kept hidden under the bed, stuff I'd witnessed in clandestine recordings downloaded from the internet, dreams, nightmares. A pure infantile fantasy: you are who you are. Your parents can go to a lot of trouble during your childhood to wipe out certain characteristics and encourage the development of others. But there are things you can't eradicate: some of us are born with fluorescent fingernails. One among a hundred, one in a thousand, one in a million. Now, nobody has to know about it; the combination of two <<D>> agents in a compound injection inhibits the organic production of lucipherase for ninety days. By this means, achieving effective negation is relatively simple, requiring only self-discipline and money. Natural selection can be bought at the corner drugstore. That's why Mama can't understand how an insignificant biological defect could have changed me into someone so different from the personality prototype she and Papa imagined for me.

An insignificant biological defect?

Imagine how it feels to see your fingernails glow in the dark, to discover that you are the result of an attempt at extermination that supposedly never happened. Having to remember night after night the years that your grandparents, along with another six million idealists, invested in collecting from garbage dumps recordings buried in the shells of old computers, all in order to manufacture a damned map of human memory, which in the end only left behind nursery rhymes for producing insomniac children

After predicting the attacks of 7/12, the group of data collectors was pursued and captured by the authorities. Someone had to be blamed for what happened on July twelfth. The prisoners were classified as conspirators and their names added to the list of subjects for experimentation, along with the demented, the freaks, the handicapped, criminals, and the homeless. The cities involved in the war among corporations contented themselves with having a scapegoat to blame. Nobody ever pointed a finger at those people who'd done nothing to prevent the dispute from exploding in the first place. Of the caged prisoners, only one group managed to escape when the laboratories became the enemy's preferred targets. According to my grandpa, this group included those who, during the incarceration, had envisioned a plan for the future. What this plan was, my grandpa never told us—although I've harbored my own suspicions for a long time. To be exact, for nineteen years, four months, and nine days. That is to say, since the last time any of the people closest to the survivors heard anything from them. For the rest of the city's inhabitants, it was only a week in which the tabloid headlines focused on profiting from the series of blackouts and strange visions experienced by city dwellers one Tuesday the nineteenth at nightfall.

Science magazines still publish articles attempting to correlate rumors about the experiments practiced for years on humans with the appearance of the swarms of electric fireflies that now make our metropolis world famous. Experts qualify this phenomenon as a resultant mutation, similar to what occurred in field mice in Chernobyl, the epicenter of the biggest nuclear disaster in history. Research conducted in the area concluded that the magnitude of evolutionary change experienced by these animals after the accident was greater than that experienced by many species in ten million years. In an analysis of just one shared gene in nine mice collected within a restricted thirty-kilometer radius in Ukraine, forty-six mutations were detected.

The hour of the fireflies has become the city's major tourist attraction. Visitors from all over the globe pay exorbitant premiums to rent rooms with views of the street. They order room service and wait for nightfall to witness the spectacle of luminous swarms that take over the avenues at that strange hour when daylight fades but it's not yet night. The glowing insects fly through the streets in one of the most beautiful natural displays on the planet, one which can only be appreciated from behind a car windshield or through an apartment window: a single electrical discharge is sufficient to wipe out three people. The fireflies' journey always ends at the same point: the entrance to the aging building which in its day housed the laboratories for human experimentation.

You know the first time the swarm of fireflies were seen

to appear in the avenues? Nineteen years, four months, and nine days ago. The same late Tuesday afternoon when all the survivors went out on the streets, leaving the doors to their homes open behind them. The few witnesses who have dared to speak swear to have seen them disappear like soap bubbles in the midst of the crowd. I's an open secret; the hypothesis goes round that the authorities back then paid off columnists in all the major newspapers to insist on how incredible and absurd these testimonies were, in order to avert an outbreak of mass hysteria in the city.

Many times I envied those who latched onto the lack of proof about the existence of the laboratories to theorize that the rumor of human experimentation was only the outlandish notion of someone with too much time on his hands; that people are simply incapable of committing that kind of atrocity against our own species; that in a hyper-connected world, reports of such a brutal circumstance would spread across the planet in minutes and the collective voice would have intervened to put a stop to something so monstrous. Perhaps. My grandpa used to say that the few times he found the strength to relate his experiences to a handful of strangers, he only prompted laughter: nobody ever believed him. The group of survivors was silently reintegrated into society. The transition was discreet; so much so that, after the peace treaty was signed between the corporations, those who were never involved in the experiments put it all down to myth: the evocation of a fluorescent scientific fantasy.

Were it not for the glow of my fingernails beneath the sheets—since I was conceived as a "little accident," by which name my father sometimes used to call me—maybe I'd have come to the same conclusion.

In front of the doors to the building, nervous laughter assaults me. Against every urban code of survival with which I've been indoctrinated, I've abandoned everything. In years past, the mere thought of experiencing something like this would have taken my breath away. I know some influential people; if I wanted, they could get me hired tomorrow by another company manufacturing self-seeded digital noise. I'd endure daily shifts of repetitive tasks, I'd collect a biweekly check I could use to hold on to my apartment, I'd complain about my cubicle, and every morning on my way to work, I'd ask myself why it's so easy to perceive when other people go insane. Last year I witnessed four jumps from the upper stories of this building. That set off my fondness for sugar cookies before bed.

I know a desperate mind is capable of convincing itself of anything, but this is different. For hours I haven't stopped hearing a determined voice repeating to me that my "biological defect" has a meaning: my purpose is to preserve human memory. Experts call it selective acceptance of reality: if you don't believe something exists, you can't see it. But, if you believe it exists. . . .

I only have to get over my fear and go outside. That's all. Once I'm there, in the middle of the crowd, I'll disappear like a bubble of soap.

Waiting

ILIANA ESTAÑOL

Translated by JOANNA TILLEY

For Doña Elena Vidal Nieto de Estañol

എ

Silverio

"WHAT WERE YOU thinking, dying here by my side in the middle of the highway? Damn it, Fermín! The plan was to make it all the way." I tried to continue driving, but my hands were sweating and slipping off the steering wheel. I wiped my hands on my pants, but they quickly grew wet again. I turned on the radio to the last station on the AM dial, Fermín's favorite, but it only made me tenser. I tried to think of what I should do, but I was so agitated that I felt soon I would join Fermín wherever he was. Through the rearview mirror I saw a patrol car behind me. It was moving slowly. It seemed like it wasn't in a hurry. But it made me think, what if they ask me to stop and they see the body? How would I explain what I was doing? I tried to drive calmly, but I felt as if my heart were leaping out of me. I turned off the road. Checking the rearview mirror, I saw that now there was no one behind me. I stopped the car, and I turned toward the backseat. There was Fermín: lying down with his eyes open. I got out of the car and observed his body for a moment. He looked relaxed, in peace. I closed his eyes. I never thought I'd be closing a dead man's eyes, let alone my own brother's.

I thought that the most sensible thing was for Fermín to sit beside me, that way no one would suspect anything. I pulled Fermín out, slowly. Then I tried to open the passenger-side door, but I couldn't while sustaining his body. After a few tries, I laid Fermín on the floor, opened the car door and hoisted him up until he was sitting in the passenger seat. But Fermín wouldn't stay seated upright. I had to secure him with the seat belt so that he wouldn't fall over. When I was finally able to close the door, I got into the car as quickly as I could. I wanted to get going before someone saw us. When I turned on the car, I realized that I didn't know where to go. I didn't know what to do. I observed my brother. He looked calm. It was as if he knew he was in good hands.

"I'm sorry, Fermín, but I'm going to have to take you back to Mexico City. Please forgive me."

Adela

THE AFTERNOON BREEZE started to air out the house, carrying away the veil of heat that smothered everything. The sound of the telephone broke the monotone tranquility of the house by the abandoned harbor. It rang various times until Adela heard it and went to answer it. She was soaked because she had been washing clothes. On the other line a voice emerged, like that of a child, distant and sad.

"Adela? It's me, Silverio. It happened too soon."

Distracted, she responded, "What happened too soon?"

Silverio remained quiet for a few seconds until he said:

"My brother, Fermín, died. I wanted to take him to the harbor, so he could die there, in his hometown. It was his last wish. I promised to take him, you know, but I never thought he would die on me along the way. I'm just an hour outside of Mexico City. If I go back there, his children aren't going to let me take him to his hometown. But if I keep on driving to the harbor, they'll resent me for traveling thirteen hours with his dead body in the car."

He stopped talking while he considered the best way to continue. Adela waited.

"So I wanted to ask you if I can take him to your house today. . . and tomorrow we can say that he died there."

She didn't answer right away.

"Uh, I don't know. I'll have to ask my aunt Esther."

Esteban

AT NINETY-EIGHT, my grandmother Esther was still extraordinarily perceptive. She spent her life traveling, visiting her family scattered throughout Latin America. Wherever she went it only took her a few days to organize her life, to get a job, a house, and friends whom it seemed she had known her whole life. But ten years ago the idea occurred to her that death was lingering, and she went back to her hometown, never to move again. Fear overwhelmed her, and she didn't even want to leave her own house. Since then I've made it a habit to come each year to visit her. I came to believe that, if I didn't come, she would die of sadness. I realized later that, perhaps, I would be the one to die if my visits to her were suspended. Her outbursts of laughter, her swearing, and her stories had become fundamental in my life. I was already accustomed to taking the bus from Mexico City. Fourteen hours of travel to arrive at the harbor that was once massive and now seems like a fragile memory. I was exhausted but always happy to be able to see her at last. When descending from the bus, a tropical heat enveloped my body and I felt at home, even though I never lived there and even though I'm really not from there. I would walk down the street that leads to the central park, strolling slowly, reacquainting myself with my surroundings, wondering where my fascination with this empty, forgotten town came from. When I arrived at my grandmother's house, I was already soaked with sweat. I grew excited at the sight of Adela and her jumping dogs on the other side of the fence, and I ran the remaining half block to get to her house. I greeted Adela and then I dodged the dogs on my way to my grandmother's room. I opened the door and greeted her warmly.

"It's high time you came back," she told me.

I found her lying down in her bed. Strangely, she lay in the opposite position from the normal one: with her feet positioned by the headboard and her head at the foot of the bed.

When I asked her why she was lying down like that, she told me, unhesitatingly, "Because the headboard is farther away from the door, and, when I die, I want my head to be the first part of my body they carry out. I don't want to leave my room feet first."

"Oh, Grandma, you and your weird ideas."

I started to sing her a song imitating a Chinese opera. It would be better described as shrieking rather than singing. She started to laugh. It was amazing to see my grandmother, so elderly, laughing wholeheartedly. Later she told me, while still laughing,

"I missed you coming over here and pestering me."

Adela entered the room hastily and asked me,

"Did your grandmother tell you?"

"What?"

"That they're going to bring a dead body here in a little bit."

She told me so nonchalantly that I didn't quite know how to react.

"No, but whose body arewe talking about?"

"An acquaintance of your grandmother," Adela responded.

My grandma looked at me with a peculiar gaze: the look of a child awaiting the reaction of an adult so as to take advantage of the opportunity to laugh, or beg forgiveness, or admit defeat.

"It's that the poor fellow died before getting here," she said coyly.

"But a dead body! What kind of mess are you getting yourselves into?" I asked as seriously as I could.

My grandma responded curiously:

"You know, the other day Doña Victoria told me that in a town near the mouth of the river, they've just built a new cemetery. The problem is they don't have any bodies to inaugurate the cemetery with, so they had to come here, asking around, wanting to know if we had any bodies to lend them."

Adela chimed in, "In that case, why don't we send them the one that's on its way here? If they're so desperate for bodies that they have to borrow them, I'm sure they'd be more than happy to accept our donation."

Such was the discussion, when the doorbell rang. Adela went immediately to the door ,and I stayed put, not knowing what to do. Without hesitation, I turned off the light and hid behind the door. Adela left, and just as I was going to show myself, she returned with a male guest. They were carrying a sack with blankets wrapped around it. I was nervous, it was the first time I had seen a dead body. I tried to keep quiet, but one of Adela's dogs came over and it started to sniff me. I had to push it away. The man glanced toward the door, where I was hiding, while he placed the dead body on the center table.

"Is Esther awake?"

Adela answered him while she cleared the glasses that were next to the sack.

"Yes, but her grandson is here too."

"What?" the man said, alarmed.

I took advantage of the confusion to appear before them as if nothing had happened. The man looked at me, and I told him good afternoon. He approached me and I held out my hand. I told him that my name was Esteban. He returned my gesture, and he told me that his name was Silverio. Adela uncovered the body while Esteban and I exchanged greetings.

"Now what do we do?" asked Adela.

When I saw the dead body it surprised me. Even though I knew it was there, it's not the same to know something as to see it. He appeared asleep and very much at peace. The strange part was that, even though he was lying on the center table, his legs were stiffly bent upwards. It took me a moment to realize that his legs were in the sitting position, suspended in the air, but still sitting. Adela attempted to rearrange the body, while saying:

"Let's lie him down more comfortably."

Silverio tried to help her, but they couldn't adjust his posture.

I realized that the blanket was caught on one of the chairs. I felt obligated to help them, and I began to approach the body, but Adela said that we should put him in bed. I protested. I reminded them that that was where my grandmother was. But it was too late. Adela led the way. When we entered my grandmother's room, she stared at the body very attentively without saying anything. We placed him on the opposite side of the bed from where she was. My grandmother, struggling to sit up, said:

"Oh, how nice that Fermín made it."

Esther

I WAS STRAINING to hear the voices in the dining room. No one had mentioned Fermín, but I knew that he had arrived already. When they entered the room, I grew excited. It had been a long time since I had seen him last, and he and I were always very good friends. They brought him to the bed and tried to lay him down, but he was stuck in a sitting position. Rigor mortis had set in. Silverio mentioned that they would have to break his bones. I refused to let them do it. I told them that he was always sitting on the porch of his house, which was his favorite position, and if he had chosen that position we would have to respect it. Everyone looked at me with surprise, and Silverio intervened with the information that that was not the position he had chosen. Fermín died lying down, and Silverio himself was the one who put him in that position. I grew angry, and I told him that if he hadn't chosen that position, then that position had chosen him, and that was the way he must remain. I would not permit them to break his bones. I neglected to tell them, however, that ever since I had fallen and broken my hip bone, I had been having recurring nightmares about the terrifying sound of bones breaking. These nightmares occurred not too often; but, when they mentioned the idea of breaking Fermín's bones, the horror from my nightmares came flooding back to me. I had a flashback to the moment of my fall, as if I were reliving it all over again. I cut my reverie short and protested again: "No way, he's staying just the way he is!" Silverio tried to reason with me, saying that there weren't coffins for people in sitting positions and that it had to be done. Esteban, noticing how troubled I was, suggested that they could give him a bath of hot water to try to loosen up his joints. He had studied medicine, which is probably why no one argued with him when he invented that preposterous idea. Adela took a bucket and went to the bathroom to fill it. As they were preparing everything, they left me alone with Fermín, sitting in his favorite position. His back was facing me, so I had to make quite an effort to stand up and go around the bed to sit beside him. He looked younger than I.

"Oh, Fermín, you're a lucky man. For so long I've waited here with the certainty that death was coming for me. But what's the use of waiting when death always comes without a warning? In fact, I'm beginning to suspect that death has forgotten all about me." I took him by the hand. It was stiff and cold. I was overwhelmed with sadness, and my eyes filled with tears. It had been many years since I had cried.

Adela

EVER SINCE FERMÍN was brought to our house that afternoon, my aunt Esther changed completely. She never divulged the secret of how she had made Fermín's "sitting legs" match the prone position of his body without breaking his bones. We had left them alone to heat up the water, and after a while, when we came back, he was already lying down in bed, perfectly straight from head to toe, and she by his side. When we asked her how she did it, all she said was that it had been over half a century since she had lain in the same bed with a man. Before we carried Fermín out, she fixed his shirt and brushed his hair. After the funeral, she started to say that she wanted to get out of the house again. The fear had left her. She wanted to go and visit her friends, to see the ocean and the river. I reluctantly informed her that almost all her friends had died, including those who where twenty or twenty-five years younger than she. But that didn't seem to dissuade her. After a few days of traveling around town, visiting tombs and relatives of friends whom we had never met before, she asked me to take her to El Brujo Beach. That was her ultimate desire. We took a taxi because she didn't want to go with anyone else. When we arrived, it surprised me to see two palm trees in the ocean, standing very upright. She also looked at them for a long time. Then she told me that the water was devouring the earth, that when she was a little girl the beach extended past those two palm trees. She asked me to undress her. It wasn't quite warm enough and I worried she might catch cold. But when she gets an idea in her head, she demands obedience. I undressed her completely, with the exception of her diaper. Without a word, she took her walker and started ambling toward the ocean. Her body appeared especially fragile against that immensity of the harbor. "Shit, she's going to die on me and then what will I do?" I said to myself. I thought about Silverio and how Fermín had died on him in similarly awkward circumstances. Fermín had obliged Silverio to bear witness to his death. Maybe I was jumping to conclusions about Esther's intentions, but at that moment it seemed quite plausible. I went over to her and tried to convince her to desist. She told me that she needed to go on alone: that she was talking to her dearly departed, to all the dead that the ocean and the earth had swallowed up, particularly my deceased mother. I backed away a few meters. But I stayed attentive in case she tried something foolish. My anxiety was heightened by the fact that even though I had grown up on the banks of the Grijalva River, very close to the ocean, I had never learned to swim. To make matters worse, the waters had taken my mother from me, forty years ago, when I was just a girl. My mother was Esther's sister. I think that's why she loved me so much. She knew that what united us was a grief larger than any love. The ocean roared, and it seemed like the voices of multitudes inhabiting the water. I closed my eyes and tried to remember my mother. My attempts were in vain, as always. I couldn't remember her face. For some reason, I thought I might have better luck being so near the water. When I opened my eyes, my aunt was staring at me. Her eyes were swollen with tears and she said:

"All right, let's go now."

We walked away slowly, and I felt as if we were two defeated soldiers, returning after losing everything. I took off her diaper, wet from the ocean, and dressed her in her dry clothes. She continued gazing at the palm trees. I told her to wait for me there, that I was going to hail a taxi. I didn't want to leave her alone, but no car was ever going to drive by that remote place. I had to run quite a distance before I found a free taxi. When I got in, I ordered him to drive as quickly as possible to El Brujo Beach. She remained there, so fragile, so alone, so sad, waiting for me in the sand. We helped her into the taxi. She was cold. When we arrived home, I laid her down and served her hot tea. I caressed her face, and she took my hand and squeezed it hard. After a while, she said,

"Adela, it seems that death hasn't forgotten about me after all."

Hunting Iguanas

HERNÁN LARA ZAVALA

Translated by EDUARDO JIMÉNEZ MAYO

ঌ৯

T HROUGHOUT THE SUMMER
my friends and I would set off early in the morning to hunt
iguanas in the highlands. I had come to the town of Zitilchén
on vacation, far from the city where my parents and I lived. My
grandparents were always willing to host me at their humble
country property. On the morning in question my friend Chidra,
of Mayan descent, was on his way down from the outskirts of
town where the highlands approach the edge of the hamlet. He
was headed toward Crispín's house, our mutual friend. On his
arrival he let out sharp whistle: calling for short, skinny Crispín

to join him. The two set out together toward my grandparents' house. Along the way they paused to collect the stones that would be used in the slingshots with which we would carry out the hunt.

Chidra filled the air with his characteristic whistle when he and Crispín reached my grandparents' farm. My grandfather went out to the gate to invite them in. Chidra had come from far off and most certainly had not eaten breakfast. His journey must have begun before sunrise. Not so for Crispín, who lived only a short distance away and always arrived well-fed. Despite the marked difference in their degree of hunger, my friends accepted with equal enthusiasm the hot chocolate and cookies that my grandmother offered them. While we ate, my tall, lanky grandfather, with his characteristic lightheartedness, took advantage of the opportunity to kid with us, especially with Crispín. The old man had always felt a special affection for him. He addressed him as Don Crispín and never hesitated to encourage him to pursue one of the myriad professions he thought would be suitable for him. "Don Crispín, have you ever considered becoming a soldier? Why, you have just the right build for it!" At that, little Crispín chuckled, revealing the cookie crumbles lodged between his teeth. Chidra took no notice of his surroundings, busy as he was stuffing himself unceremoniously with cookies and hot chocolate. My grandfather rarely addressed Chidra. The only comment he ever made about him that comes to mind was addressed principally to Crispín. Not long after hearing one of Father García's especially tendentious sermons, my grandfather mentioned to Crispín that he would probably be well-suited for many occupations but not for the priesthood. The priesthood, he said, disfavored men of a practical bent, such as Crispín. It was better suited to the likes of Chidra. I cannot remember how Chidra responded, but I suspect that he had not been paying much attention to the conversation.

We invariably left my grandparents' house at an hour much later than that which we had planned. The genteel old man always accompanied us to the gate. Our appearance, as we marched away, hardly ever varied. Chidra wore short pants, handed down to him from his older brother. Crispín and I wore long pants, purchased especially for us. Since Crispín was the smallest of the three, however, his physique prompted all sorts of jests about his frailty.

We hunted iguanas with a fair amount of regularity. But make no mistake about it: they are not an easy catch. The natural hues of the Yucatan jungle hide these reptiles as if they and their surroundings were intimate accomplices. We managed to actually catch an iguana only on the rarest of occasions. At such times we descended from the highlands jubilantly and sold our catch to that famous eatery known as the Xanadu. Turtledoves, wall lizards, and armadillos make for a much easier catch than iguanas, to give the reader a frame of reference.

That morning, as we advanced, we aimed our slingshots in the direction of anything substantial stirring in the brush, without ever striking our elusive targets or knowing if we had guessed correctly as to their presence. Chidra, who before his elders rarely divulged a word, assumed a completely distinct personality when he was with us in the highlands of the Yucatan. He became a consummate storyteller, ceaselessly spinning yarns about the fantastic adventures he had supposedly undergone during his extensive journeys in the jungle. Crispín chided Chidra mercilessly about the absurdity, stupidity, and downright impossibility of the contents of his tales. One of Chidra's most fantastical stories recounted how a parade of elephants had made its way through the highlands before his very eyes.

"That must have been the same day you drank coffee for the first time," remarked Crispín sarcastically. "I remember how you downed three or four cups in a row before you started bouncing off the walls."

But Chidra took no notice of his critic. He kept telling his tales as easily as they came to him, each one more fantastical than the next. Chidra swore, for example, that one evening after having seen a movie in town, on the way back home, certain sounds began to emerge from the brush, calling to him, "psst . . . psst." But he forced himself to ignore them since he suspected that they emanated from the Xtabay, the sinister femme fatale of Mayan mythology. He claimed that the Xtabay, having the torso of a goddess but the legs of an allegorical creature, employed her captivating voice to lure men to their doom. One of her favorite tricks involved hiding among the five-leaved silk-cotton trees and using her charming voice to lure men deeper and deeper into the thickets until they became irremediably lost. We had heard tales of the Xtabay before, but Chidra told them with such conviction that Crispín was the only boy in town who did not listen to them in awestruck silence. Chidra's imagination knew no bounds. He boasted once of having discovered a hole in the jungle floor that led effectively to the molten core of the center of the Earth. Another of his favorite yarns concerned the legendary children of Zintzinito, errant souls who appeared in the most unlikely places before vanishing without a trace.

On this particular hunt, Chidra swore to us that the very day before, while searching for his father (a rubber tapper by trade) deep in the highlands, he had seen a naked woman of majestic proportions bathing in a lake: to which Crispín, with a mixture of contempt and curiosity, responded, "I suppose you're going to swear she was the Xtabay."

"Not exactly," he said. "The Xtabay has the body of a woman and the feet of a rooster. But the woman I saw yesterday had the most beautiful white feet imaginable, long blond hair, and the body of a goddess."

"Have you ever told a true story in your life?" inquired Crispín. "If so, it's not this one for sure."

"I swear on my soul," said Chidra, making the sign of the cross and kissing the gap between his thumb and bent index finger.

"When exactly did you see her?" I demanded.

"At noon."

"The Xtabay would never show herself in broad daylight," I said.

"Enough chitchat," interrupted Crispín. "Let Chidra lead the way to the spot where he claims he saw her, and we'll put his tale to the test for once."

"That's fine with me," retorted Chidra, "but I should warn you that it's far from here, deep in the jungle."

"I knew he'd chicken out once we asked him to prove it," alleged Crispín.

"If you insist, then I'll take you," said Chidra.

Chidra knew the highlands better than any of the boys in town, not only because he lived on the outskirts but because his father could be found in the jungle on any given day tapping rubber, and Chidra's responsibilities included bringing him food and drink, and anything else he might require.

Naturally, once we had penetrated the jungle beyond the usual boundaries, Chidra assumed the task of guiding us. The town and country properties had long since faded from view. The jungle enshrouded us. We pushed our way through the thickets, treading carefully. Chidra, scouring the terrain, writhed though the jungle like a predator. Every so often, he spoke: "Over here, this way."

Something was amiss. Summer skies in the Yucatan tend to be clear, blue, and sultry, but that morning the sky was overcast. Just when the vegetation had grown so dense that we were on the verge of losing sight of the misty sky above, we came to a clearing in the brush, and an ancient Mayan sacred site emerged before our astonished eyes. It had been abandoned long ago, but its temples remained in impeccable condition. Crispín and I stood there, enthralled.

"We're close now, this way," commanded Chidra, breaking the spell that had overcome Crispín and me.

My eyes met those of Crispín. A mixture of fear and fascination united us. Chidra could wait no longer. He took the lead through the thickets, vigorously hacking away at the vegetation with his hands. All thought of hunting iguanas had vanished from our minds. The slingshots and stones in our pockets ceased to make their presence felt. All our senses were attuned to the task of discovering whether Chidra's story could possibly be true. We soon discerned the lake of which Chidra had spoken. We occupied a perfect vantage point in the thickets from which we could not be spotted. Time passed. No one appeared. Chidra's imagination, it seemed, had produced the only beauty ever to have bathed in that lake. Crispín, repeatedly accusing Chidra of being a contemptible liar, insisted that we turn back. His altercation with him was on the verge of turning violent when a person appeared at the opposite end of the lake and we all fell silent.

Not a woman, unfortunately, but a man appeared: middle-aged, dressed as an explorer, blond, graying beard, bespectacled,

smoking a pipe. A frying pan in hand, he headed toward the
basin where he squatted and set himself to washing the object in
the water. Just as he was finishing, a woman appeared, similarly
dressed, carrying more dishware. We could see them perfectly,
but we could not make out what they were saying.

"That's her! There she is!" Chidra exclaimed.

As much as we hated to admit it, it was true. Chidra had described her, in her absence, just as she appeared before us that
fateful morning: tall, white, blonde and divine. Once she had
finished cleaning her utensils, she arose and disappeared from
view to the place from where she had come.

"What the hell is making me itch so bad?" asked Crispín,
abruptly, raising his shirt to show us where it hurt.

"Ticks," said Chidra.

"Goddamn it," Crispín replied, unbuttoning his shirt.

"If you've got them then so do we," said Chidra, scrutiniz-
ing his ankles and scratching away. Chidra took off his shirt in
imitation of Crispín.

I followed suit without a thought. The three of us stripped
nude. We examined our clothes, shaking them violently to rid
them of the ticks. There must have been as many ticks on our
clothes as on our bodies. The vermin had even nestled in poor
Crispín's armpit hair. We were infested with them—on our
backs, necks, legs. In the midst of our agony, however, Chidra
surprised us by returning to the subject of the lady of the lake.
More confident than ever in his narrative's credibility, he retold
the tale of how, while venturing through the jungle in search
of his father, he had sighted the lady, completely nude, blonde,
bathing her divinely white flesh in plain view of his ravenous
but imperceptible gaze. Completely absorbed in this erotic
fable, I noticed—first to my shame, then to my relief—that we

all had begun to manifest outward signs corresponding to the rising flame within us.

Still crawling with ticks but thoroughly exhausted, we finally headed back to town. By the time we arrived, it was well past sunset. We said our farewells, and I passed through the gate of my grandparents' farm. I opened the front door to the house, my eyes heavy with drowsiness. My thoughts remained with the lady of the lake, but my body no longer responded to her, rather to the itch of the vermin, which had taken possession of it.

I hurried to my grandmother and complained about the ticks that besieged me. She helped me undress and remove the vermin while simultaneously making light of my anguish: "They're ticks, not black widows!" Realizing that stronger measures might be required to achieve complete victory over the vermin and to set my mind at ease, she hastened to the kitchen to heat some wax. Obeying her orders, I awaited her in bed.

I lay face down on the bed while my grandmother applied hot wax to my back and asked me: "What the devil were you boys up to today?"

"Today we saw the Xtabay, Grandma," I answered contentedly.

1965

EDMÉE PARDO

Translated by LESLY BETANCOURT-GONZÁLEZ

For my sister

❧

I<small>N</small> 1965 THE SPACECRAFT *Mariner 4* passed Mars, taking pictures of the red planet, and the world—well, a part of the world—was astonished by the images. In Mexico City, the same year and month, Ángel Márquez, judo instructor, enthusiastically summoned his students with great hopes for progress and achievement. One can imagine their white suits, black belts, serious composure, and graceful movements patterned after the motions of crickets and other natural creatures. In that same fringe neighborhood, known as Echegaray, far from the eyes of God, my mother was befuddled by her second child, myself, a newborn girl, wailing for milk, while the newspapers displayed images from outer space and the cause of my father's absence since the following evening was confirmed. Meanwhile, my older sister, who really was not much older than me, being barely two at the time, was sleeping—and my mother hoped that somewhere in the universe or in the city there was peace to be found, for she longed to experience it.

My mother often spoke of peace. The television news broadcast images of Vietnam continuously, bombs, napalm, and such, while "I pray for peace, to be at peace, a world at peace" were phrases that constantly passed through my mother's lips. Peace has never played a central role in my life. Since my birth there have been wars in every corner of the planet. In the movies, cities and entire nations are annihilated with the push of a button, and spaceships are blasted out of existence with the most sophisticated technology. Nonetheless, the war for peace continues to be waged in my mother's heart and in the hearts of many others. I have never known substantial peace, since my life has transpired in the shadow of paternal absence, war, pugnacious politicians, negligent martial arts instructors, and my mother's endless troubles.

When I started elementary school and learned that there was another student named Paz (Spanish for peace) in my class, I decided to make friends with her and invite her to my home, so that my mother could have what she wanted most in life: and what she sometimes found in the tiny sleeping pills in a bottle which she desperately withdrew from her bureau drawer.

"My mom would like you to come over for dinner," I said to Paz at recess. It was the first time we spoke.

She agreed.

"One of my friends wants to meet you. She's seen you when

you come to pick me up," I said to my mother, who smiled gratifyingly.

This is how a long-lasting friendship was initiated not only between Paz and me but also between her and my mother. To compensate Paz for the benefits she bestowed on my mother, I gave her own mother hugs full of love. Her mother's plumpness, which provoked so much ridicule in school, was a haven for me—a warm, comfortable pillow upon which I could lay my head.

Sometimes I suspected that Paz and I had been switched at birth: that her mother was biologically mine and mine was hers. Paz's mother seemed to treat me with greater tenderness than Paz, and mine seemed to treat Paz with more intimacy than she treated me; we never could figure out if it this was out of common courtesy or an expression of their true allegiances. I learned about Paz's father because of the pictures in the house, through the stories expressed in them. As it happens, her father was Ángel Márquez, a judo instructor. The martial arts and the lessons of the Toyama were unknown to me then. Its practitioners seemed like latent criminals: why else would they fight so violently? In time, I learned that the very night before the newspapers exposed the world to the first pictures of Mars from deep space, a mugging obstructed my father's presence at my birth. The image of a band of brutal men in white uniforms with black belts kicking my dad in the face entered my mind when I viewed the photograph of Paz's father, which probably explained why I disliked him without ever having met him; but the fact that he abandoned his family without warning one day, and Paz's mother never smiled again, also shaped my scornful opinion of the man.

NASA launched the *Viking 1* on a mission to Mars, inserting into the planet's orbit in 1976. Talk of Martians occupied the center of our discussions then, being of personal and collective significance to us. It was of interest to me, personally, because it was rumored that an expedition of aliens would visit the Earth when peace reigned on our planet, and my mother needed this kind of peace even more than she needed my friend Paz.

"If the Martians come, I hope they take me with them," my mother said in an unforgettably solemn tone.

"You'd really take off, just like that, and leave me behind?" I asked anxiously.

Her response mingled tenderness, disillusionment, lethargy, and curiosity. It was then that I learned of the coincidence between my birth and the first photographs from deep space of the planet Mars, which she showed me.

"I've always wondered what's up there in the sky, what the worlds beyond ours are like. But no, honey, I wouldn't leave you."

Her answer calmed me, partially, but deep down I knew that her desire to leave this world was not fleeting, and that she really wanted to know if the peace she so desired might be found in another world.

I met Ángel Márquez in person at Paz's mother's funeral. Paz and I were in college by then, and her mother's plumpness had escalated into morbid obesity. Her coffin had to be special-ordered, triple the size of the average one, to fit her entire body. Her husband, the judo instructor, looked much the same as in the photos in their family home, only smaller and thinner. I laughed at my childish presumption that Ángel Márquez, in reality so little, could have beaten up my father, big and tough both in my eyes and in reality. But my parents were already divorced by then. My mother had stopped taking pills, and it seemed that part of her inner turmoil had subsided. Apparently much of her battle was fought against my father and on his account: the love that was supposed to bring her happiness left her with two daughters and the agitation of a man who was habitually unfaithful.

Outer space and its inhabitants came back to my attention the day I heard my mother, an elder woman but not yet senile, say that she had dreamed of and believed that she had seen Martians. People eventually find what they want if they are persistent, and my mother had spoken about extraterrestrials all her life: or it was just the beginning of the decline of her mental capacities; or had life finally given her what she had wished for so long? My older sister, we were both older by then, grimaced when I told her what our mother had said. Neither of us knew what to think; but Paz, who knew her almost as well as we did and had the advantage of not being bound to her by blood, talked about the possibility that my mother's visions were real: real to her, at least. Fortunately, my mother showed no other signs of madness at that stage.

1999 came around and talk revolved around the new millennium and the possibility of the end of the world. Theories emerged from everywhere: in some there was extreme fear, in others extreme hope. The minority professed that the world would continue as it always had, while growing increasingly sophisticated. When the new millennium came with more of a whimper than a bang, the more radical theories vanished without a trace. My mother never made another comment to her daughters about the Martians, but Paz and she had long conversations about it. I neglected to mention that Paz was an avid believer in life on other worlds and in the exchange of information between them. She gleaned this from her readings rather than from experience.

It seemed normal that Paz sought out my mother more often in the wake of her mother's death; we shared the privilege of receiving my mother's love and in some ways the responsibility of caring for her as she aged. In fact, Paz probably would have moved in with her had my mother lived out the full course of her life. But what happened then, years after the new millennium, has no logical explanation; neither the police nor detectives nor clairvoyants have been able to give a reasonable account of it. One day I tried to call Paz, but she did not answer her home or cell phone. When I contacted my mother about it, she explained that Paz was going through a very hard time and had gone to her for solace. She had not mentioned anything because she did not want to alarm me. When I got there I expected to see my friend distraught and in tears, but she seemed in perfect mental health. There were books and magazines on UFOs strewn about and I arrived when they were about to watch a video on the topic. The documentary was intriguing, but I watched it with some trepidation because I was more concerned about what was happening between the two of them rather than those creatures with the huge eyes and heads. But there were no apparent clues.

"We're fine," Paz said when we embraced as I left.

I telephoned my older sister, who was beginning to act like my younger one.

"You handle it; she's your friend." And she hung up.

There was nothing wrong with them spending some quality time together, I told myself; perhaps my worrisome mind was overreacting. As a matter of fact, it was refreshing to know that my mother had someone to keep her company during the day. That is what I told myself, at least, until one afternoon no one answered the phone, no one came to the door, and when I went inside I found everything in perfect order with a letter addressed to my sister and me on the living-room table. I did not dared open it until my sister arrived. In brief, they wrote that with mutually reinforced courage they managed to communicate with the aliens, who had agreed to take them along so long as they agreed never to return to Earth. They expressed their love to everyone in their farewell statement, and with morbid humor they pointed out that at least they had saved us the expense and strain of a funeral. In the letter, Paz requested that her father be informed of her whereabouts, as if that were within the realm of possibility. We called my father and Ángel Márquez and together we examined the letter, raising questions and venturing conjectures. We called the police, a detective, and a clairvoyant, in that order, following their disappearance. No one could proffer an answer, and a full three years later we still have no explanation other than the contents of the letter. That document has driven a wedge between my sister and me and we never even see each other anymore unless it is to meet my father for dinner.

Sometimes I believe that my mother finally found peace in a world beyond our own; other times I fear that she and Paz were kidnapped and are being kept as slaves: that is, if they were not already tortured, raped, and murdered. The other morning, when I stepped out to pick up the newspaper, I noticed that the headlines referred to Mars with full-color photographs accompanying the feature story. New lenses and more precise instruments revealed figural patterns reminiscent of a human face on the surface of the planet. Some maintain that they are artifacts of an ancient civilization, but I find a striking resemblance to my mother in them.

Variation on a Theme of Coleridge

ALBERTO CHIMAL

Translated by CHRIS N. BROWN

❧

I GOT A CALL. It was me, calling from a phone I lost the year before. I asked me where I had found the phone. I answered myself that it was in such and such cafeteria that I couldn't remember anymore.

"You're sick," I said, calling from who knows where. "What have you done with your life? Still getting fat? Still stuck in your crisis?"

I told myself no, but in reality I was lying and I knew it.

"You're lying," I told myself.

"What do you want?" I asked me, a little annoyed with myself. Why was it I was looking for myself at this particular moment?

"You must be wondering why I'm looking for you right now," I said.

"It's not true!" I answered.

"The one that gets mad loses," I said, laughing at myself, and I wanted to hang up but I stopped myself, saying, "You need someone to put you in your place and straighten you out."

Then there was a knock on the door, and it turned out it was me. I'd been standing there the whole time.

"Obviously I know where you live, idiot," I said to myself without hanging up the cell phone.

"It's not worth it," I answered. "Go ahead and hang up already."

It was really ridiculous to keep talking on the cell phone. But it didn't really console me to think that, if I saw me as being ridiculous, I also saw myself as being ridiculous. In fact I wanted to cry from the realization that I actually looked younger and skinnier, and only a year had passed. Even worse, I had hair, I still had hair, when really I'd had one of my crises the day before and I'd shaven and I looked pathetic.

"You look pathetic," I said to myself. I couldn't take any more. I started to really cry, and answered me. "Yes." And then I fell to the floor. And then, against all expectations, I knelt and hugged myself, hugged myself and consoled myself and told myself that everything was going to be okay, that if I didn't help myself then who was going to help me . . . or so I told myself.

"We're going to need to hang up," I added after a moment, and laughed. I laughed too, sucking up the tears and thinking how unworthy our pose was. Then it occurred to me that I'd gotten negligent, because my telephone from a year ago was in better shape than the one I have now.

Photophobia

MAURICIO MONTIEL FIGUEIRAS

Translated by JEN HOFER

For Juvenal Acosta and Andrei Codrescu

⁂

Is that not why ghosts return:
to drink the blood of the living?

—J.M. COETZEE

THE APOCALYPSE, for him, was an everyday concern—corroborated each morning by the light which pierced his pupils with thousands of pins shot out from a mute atomic explosion the moment his eyelids opened like floodgates to scatter the water of his dreams all over the floor. The pain was so sudden, so brutal, that it forced him to close his eyes again and grope for his dark glasses on the bedside table, his pulse at a gallop and his temples pounding fiercely in prelude to a headache. Once the shades were settled—then, only then—he ventured to blink, to untangle the skein of information which his vigil cast before him. Panting and sweaty, while the phosphenes readapted themselves to the blood-red gloom out of which they had blossomed, he began the work of reacquaintance: there were his legs, joined in a mountain range tangling the sheets into peaks which angled down towards the foot of the bed, and beyond that was the profile of a chair, the dust dancing in a diagonal of sun, particles of matter concentrating around forms which would end up being the bathroom door, the curtains which did not quite cover the only window, the stains on the rug—his sense of smell, with feline keenness, detected equal parts of semen and liquor—left as a legacy by former guests. Little by little, as his eye deciphered that resplendent chaos, converting it into a legible code, he understood that the atomic explosion was simply his mind's dirty trick, part of a dream which day after day he tried in vain to reconstruct. Little by little, the sense of apocalypse was bursting into the world with its useless cargo; the omens disseminated in the press and on television were nothing compared to the ocular catastrophe to which he had been condemned for all eternity—eternity, he thought, a smile twisting his mouth, another useless word for the great dictionary of human vaguenesses. What was eternity if not the weight of the sun on his naked eyes, the seconds it took him to find his glasses on the night table, the lapse that was necessary before the phosphenes would disappear? Let's talk about eternity, he thought, addressing an invisible interlocutor; let's talk about the instantaneous blindness it has been my task to eradicate since time immemorial. Let's talk about how frustrating it is not to be able to recall the last time one awoke without fear of pain and panic about the light, without the primitive terror brought on by the first solar arrows boring through one's eyelids. Let's talk about the dark, that inverse light where our eyes ripen like slow-growing fruits.

That morning, however, he awoke with the sensation that something had happened to the light. At first it was a subtle intuition, a change in the periphery of his visual field inducing dark ruminations, a certain parsimony in the dust attracted by the ray of sun filtering in through the window. Once he had his glasses on and his breath under control, he inhaled vigorously until he thought his lungs would explode; his sense of smell, once again he could confirm it, was a reliable ally: the air was charged with an electric tension which he had only sensed on late afternoons in summer just before a deluge broke. A strange density had slipped into the atmosphere like a swarm of insects; it was, in fact, easy to hear a remote buzzing, a generator-like murmur reminiscent of thousands of elytrons soaring into the distance. He pricked up his ears. There they were as always—as every morning, as every night—the sounds which populated his auditory universe: cockroaches scurrying in the corners of the hotel, the whisper of spiders weaving their webs, the screech of rats looking for food—how many times, he thought, had his hunger impelled him to feed on them?—the mosquito's transparent song, a butterfly's rubbing against the glass, the termites' tireless litany.

Something, however, was missing in this secret world.

Birds.

The birds had hushed, contributing to the strangeness which saturated the air.

And the flies, the flies too seemed to have disappeared in pursuit of new decay.

And the smell: a mixture of ambush and emptiness, of geologic fermentations and virgin asphalt.

And the light: a thick grayish ink that oozed between the curtains and drenched the rug.

And the murmur, the remote elytrons of absence.

He leapt out of bed, his senses sharper than usual. A glance at the magazines and newspapers accumulated on the floor after a two-week confinement confirmed something that the shadows of the night had relegated to the background: the train of the century was running—and would continue running, as far as the rails would allow—towards the abyss to which a humanity run awry was driving it. As headlines and magazine covers were reporting, almost all the cars of that train had been reserved to transport baggage which was both ominous and absurd: biblical commentaries and forecasts, unrehearsed meteorological shows, an increase in the number of suicides, a boom in religious sects, a collective mania. In England, a woman had dressed her children as angels before making them swallow a poison which hadn't been heard of since the nineteenth century. In Iran, a group of young men had set a mosque on fire as part of a plot to eliminate any trace of the Muslim creed. In Australia, a tsunami known as the Last Wave had left tens of thousands dead. In Egypt, an elderly man had hung himself in his tent across from the Pyramid of Cheops with a message "for humankind" hidden in his tunic. In a small American town, organizations for Aryan purity were scheming to get rid of racial minorities "forever." In the city on the outskirts of which he was staying, an accountant had killed his immediate superior by stabbing him in the eye with a pencil. Eternity, he thought, pocket apocalypses: man has not learned the lessons of history, he is still the ignorant student who recorded his confusion in the caves of Altamira—it's just that the caves have become tabloids. The crude drawings of bison and birds and solitary, emaciated silhouettes are now the photographs of a perplexed crowd.

As he went into the bathroom, he felt the air stirring around him as if it were a robe: it was that rarefied, it was that dense. He closed the door behind himself, and once he was safely in the semi-dark, he took off his glasses, leaning into the mirror. What better light than shadow in which to face the reddened gaze of his mornings, the effects of the sun reduced to a constant trickle of tears? He grabbed one of the hundreds of bottles of eyedrops strewn about—on the sink and on the toilet, on the floor and in the shower—and dedicated himself to his daily balsam ritual: a cataract for his sick eyes, recommended by an ophthalmologist who had died a couple of months earlier. After his prescribed rubdown, he shaved, washed his face, soaped his groin, armpits and neck, and then rinsed himself. He dressed slowly, enjoying the dark friction of his clothes, which he kept in the bathroom so he could avoid encountering the morning light—years before he had decided that closets were the realm of insects—whistling the jingle from one of his favorite commercials, something about eyedrops or maybe blood donations. He combed his hair, put on deodorant, a bit of cologne, and his glasses, and he left, ready to challenge the brightness.

He drew the curtains, and the spectacle afforded by the window, though he had intuited it already, still managed to surprise him: it was the spectacle of absence. There were empty cars, doors wide open, in the parking lot and in the middle of the highway which passed in front of the hotel; the few birds— mostly crows, as far as he could see—remained motionless on the electrical and telephone wires; the flies seemed to imitate them, petrified on the gravel and the glass like fossils of an extinct species. The sky was now a kind of hospital for cloudy bellies, heavy with rain, which crept along lazily and allowed the sun's invasion only with great difficulty. Eternity, he thought, let's see what they think about this eternity.

He left the room and breathed deeply; it had been years, maybe decades since he had given himself over to the smell of desolation with such pleasure, such indolence. He began to walk through the parking lot, hearing with amplified clarity the crunch of the gravel and the hustle and bustle of the ants, examining the cars one by one. He saw trunks exhibiting their contents with an utter lack of modesty, suitcases and bags with the still-fresh prints of escape, clothes strewn on the floor recalling the installations of certain contemporary artists. He laughed at the idea. Who would have believed, only a century ago, that something so common, so anonymous as clothing, would be elevated to the status of an art object; why that modern zeal to glorify the disposable, the perishable? Before, he thought, art had boiled down to a canvas and a brush, to capturing the battle between light and shadow. Before, the body in all its irregularity was immortalized; today the wrapping counted much more, so much more that the body had disappeared. It was still there, of course, the corpus delicti: shirts and pants, blouses and skirts, shoes and sneakers—a hollow corpse. Before, he thought, immortality dressed differently.

He walked down the middle of the highway, stopping from time to time next to an empty car, letting himself be caressed by the mountain wind which hurried towards the south, when an image whirled into his mind. It was the memory—vague, intertwined with the strands of a dream—of a bustling dawn filled with voices and steps coming from all directions, motors and honking horns and doors opening—the sounds of flight, the music of involuntary exile. This memory was joined by another which planted a new smile on his lips: the cable TV pornography marathons to which he had enjoyed subjecting himself for the past few years. Far from transporting him to the orbit of onanism—the words belonged to someone he had met in one of the bars he used to frequent before he began to devote his nights to sleep—pornography amused him so much that he had come to think of it as the display which best attested to the ridiculous human parade; nothing was more comfortable than to enter a hotel room—how many had he stayed in these past months? By now he had lost count—lie back on the bed, find the remote control, and spread out the banquet of fragile, transitory flesh given over to an obviously fake frenzy. Frenzy? he thought; frenzy the blood which clambers through veins and arteries, the eyes which shrink from the sun. Frenzy that of the flesh which surrenders itself to the dark, to the fondling of eternity.

The image of three or four bodies moving like pistons in some primary machine accompanied him all the way to the tollbooths lined up perpendicular to the highway, marking the limits of the city which had sheltered him since June, and which had vanished miles ago to make way for a mountainous rural landscape—the end of civilization. The air paid his toll with its persistent whistle; the booths—he had already smelled it—were deserted. He inspected them, however, one after the other. He saw a calendar with the image of a naked woman offering her generous breasts to the spectator along with an icy blue stare. He saw a bodybuilding magazine with its pages ripped, a coffeepot filled to the brim. He saw a radio playing only static, which he decided to leave on; he thought of how lovely it would be to hear the batteries draining as the day decline,d and he regretted that he could not wait while it happened. Standing in the middle of the highway, his heart and lungs swollen with joy, he immersed himself in the morning's leaded plateau and felt, for the first time in a long while, that he could eat up—no, drink down—the world in great gulps. He then exhaled a sigh which soon became a shout of celebration, a bellow which reverberated in the distance where the city shimmered.

As if in response to the echo which remained hanging in the air, a ray of sunlight pierced the clouds and landed suddenly on a gas station located beyond the tollbooths, encircling it with a misty halo—a revelation in the confines of empty space. Dazzled, his mind become the museum where he had seen an Edward Hopper exhibit one afternoon; he let himself be drawn like a magnet towards the light which seemed to flow from one of Hopper's most desolate canvases: "Gas," if his memory didn't fail him, with its service station attended by a man in a vest, waiting for a car which might save him from paralysis. Keep waiting, he thought as he looked around; maybe someday one of those ghost cars will rescue you. After all, even immortality needs fuel.

Hurried steps—the first sign of human life in several hours—made him turn towards the gas station just as three young men were leaving the attached store carrying cans and cereal boxes. He realized that he was watching a robbery by the way they flung the packages into the trunk of the car which was waiting for them with its motor running—behind the wheel there was a fourth figure—by the look of terror that one of them gave him before shouting a warning at his companions, by the obscene finger that shot from one of the windows as the car sped towards the south, its tires screeching. What a shame, he said to himself, and shook his head as he remembered the man in Hopper's painting; maybe you'd get lucky the next time. When he got to the gas station, he kicked a box of Corn Flakes and noticed how the ray of sunlight languished, how the darkness gained territory; then, humming the theme song to an old movie, he strolled between the pumps. He saw them as an apt legacy of humanity: monoliths for a future with neither gasoline nor cars, totemic remnants of a culture which had forged its own eclipse. The fugitives' car merged into the horizon, which quickly regained its faded consistency.

The first thing that surprised him when he walked into the self-service store was its tidiness, the almost prophylactic atmosphere which reigned inside. The metal shelves, gleaming beneath buzzing lamps—his sense of smell assured him that all dust had been completely eradicated—displayed their products with an order bordering on monomania, making him think of ads, of the set for a commercial about to be filmed; from one moment to the next a man might burst in, smiling from ear to ear, with a Hopperesque vest and unleashing a string of discounts and promotions.

He wandered between the shelves, searching for some trace of the fugitives—barely even a can of Campbell's soup which he picked up and put back in its place—when his ear detected a rustling he had previously overlooked: the rubbing of fabric against a metallic surface. He crossed the labyrinth of canned goods and discovered that his imagination had not deceived him this time; standing next to the cash register at the entrance to the store, a man wearing a vest and round wire-rimmed glasses was obsessively cleaning the counter, absorbed in the cloth which traced concentric circles, the stains which he scraped at with a fingernail he then sucked, only to resume his labor. Circles and fingernail, pause, circles and fingernail—and so on until infinity, the inexorable ritual of cleanliness.

In the operating-room light of the store, the clerk shone as if they had just finished painting him, as if he had only recently emerged from a fresh canvas. Who, he thought, could have forced the man to clean forever and ever under these surgical lamps? He imagined Hopper's painting, the empty space the escaped figure would leave, the bewilderment on the face of the spectator who would make the discovery, the newspaper headlines: "Escape in the Art World," "Hopperesque Creature Flees." Who would fill that hole, what would the reward be for reporting the figure's whereabouts?

He cleared his throat and spoke to the clerk:

"How are you . . . ? Good morning."

In the silence that followed, the rubbing of the cloth seemed scandalous. Circles and fingernail, pause, circles and fingernail. The man's blood flowed with astonishing calm, immutable. Cold blood, he thought. The blood of waiting. No relation whatsoever to the warmth of fear.

"How are you?" he repeated. "How's everything going? I saw that some guys . . ."

He stopped himself when he noticed the gun resting on the counter, half hidden by the cash register, and that the man moved only to continue cleaning. Circles and fingernail. Pause. Circles and fingernail.

"Excuse me," he insisted. "Are you all right?"

Without looking up or interrupting his work, the man finally spoke. His voice was, in fact, sharp—a fingernail tracing circles on glass.

"Take whatever you need," he said. "I only ask that you don't make any mess." He paused and added: "Those fellows did as they were told, and they had knives. I told them that it had taken me hours to arrange the store, that they should take whatever they wanted. Even in shelters you have to eat, they said. I know that, I said, why? We don't have anything to pay with, they said. I know that, I said, I don't give a damn, take what you want and get the hell out of here. You aren't coming with us? they said. I can't, I said, I haven't finished cleaning." Another pause while he brought a fingernail to his mouth, and then, between his teeth: "I'll never finish . . . There's so much dirt . . ."

"And what do you want that for?" he said, pointing to the gun as he approached the counter.

As if an electrical charge had run through him, the man raised his eyes—two exhausted, reddened spheres where the spectacle of absence was reflected clearly. The rhythm of his blood continued, unchanging.

"What do I want it for . . . ?" he repeated, for himself more than anything. He let go of the cloth and began to caress the butt of the gun like a sleepwalker. "What do you think? To open the door when I finish cleaning . . . What a dumb question."

"The door . . . ?"

"My brains, all right, so you'll understand me." The man snorted and raised a fingernail to his mouth mechanically. "So that I can open them up when I finish with the stains . . . If I finish, that is. There's so much filth . . ."

The buzzing of the lamps seemed to intensify. The murmur, he thought, the elytrons of absence. Then he said:

"Is it loaded?"

The man spat out a bit of nail, which he immediately cleaned off the counter with the palm of his hand. He answered after a few seconds.

"It has two bullets . . . You know, in case something doesn't work out." After a pause he continued, in a more confidential tone: "Tell me honestly . . . Which is better: to get ahead of eternity, or to let eternity catch up with us?"

Eternity, he thought, will always find a place in a foolish conversation at the end of civilization. He saw that the man was lowering his eyes again and focusing first on the cloth and then on the gun, as if he were waiting to hear them speak at any moment.

"To get ahead of it, of course," he said, and a wary irony filtered into his words. "If eternity catches up with us there's nowhere to run."

The man smiled, a convulsive grin directed to the gun, a face crisscrossed by fearless blood.

"Yes, you're right . . . Yesterday was my one-year anniversary here. A year! No one told me that eternity lasted twelve months, that I had been hired to be the last watchman . . . Before, we watchmen guarded a tower in the desert; now we have to tend to dumps like this. The desert's changed, but the dirt hasn't, oh no, the dirt's the same, and it'll keep on being the same, eh? The invisible enemy . . . Yes, you're right: now there's nowhere to run. With so much dirt there's nothing else to do but get ahead of eternity."

The man passed a hand across his head and, with a sigh, set about his cleaning again: circles and fingernail, pause, circles and fingernail. When he spoke, his voice had regained its neutral mannequin's tone. "Take what you like, just don't mess anything up. I spent hours arranging this pile of trash." He hesitated, and then added: "Anyway, we don't accept American Express."

He said good-bye. Before leaving, he turned to look at the clerk from the doorway and found him more Hopperesque than ever, radiant beneath the surgical glare, prisoner of his own eternity. What very cold blood escapees have, he thought.

"Are you sure everything's okay?" he said.

"I'm sure," the man muttered without removing his gaze from his work. "I have to finish cleaning . . . The only thing you can be certain of is the dirt you have to watch out for."

"See you soon, then."

There was no response.

As he walked along the highway he heard the first shot clearly, a blast which fractured the morning's gray silence. Moments later the second detonation came, and the air carried it towards the distant city. In case something doesn't work out, he thought. Now I understand why a man might actually want two ounces of prevention.

When he returned to the hotel, the open doors and empty rooms confirmed that he was abandonment's only guest, the guest of honor at a ceremony which would begin shortly. He explored a few rooms, collecting their emanations and humors, constructing a mental image of their occupants: here a pair of newlyweds or perhaps lovers—the smell of sex was so intense that it almost wove a second carpet—there a woman whose child was sick with diarrhea. The front desk did not offer any further surprises; only the bell on the counter attracted his attention, calling to mind the memory of a navel he had caressed decades or eons before. In front of the pool—if that's what you could call that narrow rectangle of cloudy water—he amused himself following the trajectory of a rubber duck which the wind moved around at whim like a compass for tracking lost childhood. Then he lay down on one of the beach chairs decayed from disuse and the elements, and let himself be lulled to sleep by the insects' scurrying, by the whisper of the trees and the humidity of the air, lifting his chin as if to challenge the sun in its futile attempt to dominate the stormy sky.

Noon pulled him gradually out of his drowsiness. Dazed, he looked at the chaises around him and thought of seats readied for a journey with no return; he thought of the Hopper painting "People in the Sun," which had always disturbed him, and for a moment he believed that he had pried himself from the canvas, that he was one of the figures that the painter had sentenced to immortal stupor in beach chairs. A series of stomach growls sufficed to rid him of his laziness and remind him that he had not eaten—in a manner of speaking—for many hours now. He began to walk towards his room.

He was taking a piece of cheese and some raw meat out of the small fridge when his cell phone rang.

"Yes?" he answered. "Ah, yes . . . How are you. Yes . . . Aha . . . Of course I understand, but . . . Yes, I know that . . . Aha . . . I can imagine it perfectly, but . . . What? No, listen to me . . . Aha . . . No, no . . . Listen to me, listen to me! . . . We're all in the same boat, I've told you that a thousand times . . . No, you listen to me! . . . I'm tired of telling you that we have to be patient! . . . Patient! . . . Do you know what it is to be patient? . . . We've been patient for such a very long time, I don't know . . . What? No, no one is going to die from waiting a little longer! . . . What? Of course not! . . . I swear, I promise, whatever you want . . . Patience, goddammit! . . . Why are you in such a rush? . . . What? Yes . . . You'll see, you'll see . . . Just so it's clear: without patience there is nothing, nothing . . . All right . . . Calm down . . . What? No, calm down . . . See you soon."

He hung up and took a few swigs from the bottle of whiskey on the night table to wash down his rage and desperation. Okay, he said to himself, take it easy. While he ate lunch, he remembered, not without a certain fury, the calls from all over the world which he had had to answer, to tolerate, over the past few days; all of them, without exception, focused on the same question: when, *when?* They're like children, he thought, spoiled children utterly ignorant of the ancestral art of patience. So many years of stoic waiting about to be thrown overboard merely because of their inability to endure a little while longer. As if I weren't just like them, he thought, as if I had not initiated them on this path made of patient steps. As if my eyes didn't burn each morning.

To distract himself he took another long swig from the bottle, picked up the remote control and turned on the television; a roar of static fractured the apparent stillness. He turned down the sound and flipped through the local and cable channels. The spectacle of absence repeated itself over and over again: a gray tempest, a cathodic hissing which set his nerves on edge. The few stations which had not yet gone off the air were broadcasting similar images: maps of different cities crowded with symbols indicating the locations of nuclear shelters. Only on CNN did he encounter a space where the real world—a memento of the real world—insinuated itself timidly: a studio inhabited only by screens and consoles which blinked in desolation, waiting for newscasters who had forgotten their papers on the varnished desk in the foreground. Eternity, he thought, who would report the news of eternity, of so many thirsty shadows? He turned off the TV, and, after making sure that the curtains were drawn, after leafing for the umpteenth time through the magazines and newspapers strewn about the floor, he determined that the best way to kill time was drinking—whiskey, for now. With the half-full bottle in his hand, he tumbled onto the bed. Cheers, he murmured. Cheers and *Laus Deo*.

A hangover, barely a soft veil against his temples, woke him hours later; three aspirins and a little cocaine were enough for him to shake it off. Though the late afternoon had already turned into a night as dense as the day, disturbed by flashes of lightning and infused with an oily atmosphere bristling with electricity, he decided to keep his dark glasses on. And now that he had recovered his good mood, thanks to his nap, he turned on the television only to confirm that the world—even on CNN—had dissolved beneath an avalanche of dirty snow. What a way to celebrate the broadcasting apocalypse, he thought, with a great feast of invisibility crowned at the last moment with static. He went to pee, realized he had one last sip of whiskey left, turned off his cell, which was ringing insistently, grabbed the only chair in the room and prepared himself to wait in the hallway of the hotel. To wait, he thought, one must know how to wait, like the creatures on Hopper's chaises, like the men in vests at the borders of civilization; in the end, we're all just looking out for dirt. He noticed that the wind whipped the doors of the vacant rooms, a noise that had filtered into his nap in the form of fluttering wings. Birds, he thought, that's why I dreamt a rainstorm of birds. He studied the electrical wires and phone lines; the crows had disappeared without a trace. The highway appeared to vibrate, swaddled in an illumination which seemed to him false, like that of a puppet theater. The city was nothing more than a faraway book in which the storm recorded its scribbles of light.

His watch read eleven forty-three when the blackout occurred. Preceded by a clap of thunder which shook the air, the ground, the entire world, with vertiginous speed the darkness gained more and more territory: first the hotel, which seemed to fall into an endless pit, and after a few seconds the highway, which dragged with it cars and tollbooths alike as it fell. Free of earthly brightness, the sky imposed itself abruptly onto the landscape: a violet-colored belly, swollen, run through with white veins.

Captive to a childish excitement, he got up from his chair and walked through the parking lot until he was able to catch sight of the city which twinkled—which had been twinkling—in the distance which was now conquered by darkness. It's always good to come home, he thought. Whoever says that in the beginning was the Word is wrong: there is no origin other than the Dark. *Wilkommen, bienvenue, welcome,* he hummed, *to our cabaret, our cabaret, our cabareeeeet.* Welcome, ladies and gentlemen, to the show of darkness; hopefully you will not find it too inconvenient. Children, my dear children, he thought, our wait has ended, it's time to get drunk. He laughed, and, still without giving up his glasses—he had the sense that they sharpened his vision somehow, darkness on darkness—he skipped onto the highway and began to slide down the asphalt to the rhythm of a Viennese waltz which flooded his mind. A little, he said to himself as he danced, just a little more.

It happened moments after midnight fell against the world with its entire weight. The air, before anything else the air: one instant it was whistling and the next it became completely paralyzed. Then the change in the atmosphere, a kind of swift compression, as if enormous hands were wringing it, reducing it to a ball of extraordinary density. Then the earthquake above his head and under his feet, a jolt which united the sky and the earth into one single trembling organ. And then, in the middle of the pristine silence which flowed out in all directions, the light: the most clear, the most beautiful, the sun of suns, its glow stoking the cosmos to its farthest corner. And after that the clamor, an avalanche of sound which buried even the music of the heavens.

Unmoving in the middle of the highway, all his senses aroused to their very limits, his lips twisted into a smile which grew second by second, he closed his eyes. When he opened them he could not avoid the flashing in his memory of Hiroshima and Nagasaki, the Nevada desert, the Pacific atolls; the mushroom cloud—slender, gorgeous—which rose up on the horizon as if of its own accord, was the irrefutable proof that humankind was—and would continue to be, as far as the nuclear shelters would allow—the same humankind of long ago. No one, he thought, would have believed that man could make such sublime mushrooms blossom.

As he turned towards the lair which some nights before he had dug in the damp soil at the back of the hotel, he imagined pupils exposed to the apocalypse that he had evaded for centuries, hands covering eyes forced to witness the spectacle of bones through radiographic skin, bottles of eyedrops at the moment of dissolution. As he took off his dark glasses, he imagined his children, his beloved progeny, repeating that same gesture all over the world, and he pictured himself walking together with them along highways sown with eyeglasses. He recalled the temperature human blood reached when fear took root, and he could do nothing more than cluck his tongue.

Wilkommen, bienvenue, welcome, he thought, to real live eternity—a time dedicated to drink. Or was that not why they, ghosts, always returned: to drink the blood of the living few?

The Last Witness to Creation

JESÚS RAMÍREZ BERMÚDEZ

Translated by EDUARDO JIMÉNEZ MAYO

For Enrique, Mario, Fernando, Chucho, and Paul

ఴ

J ANUARY 12, 1999. A patient hands me this note: *I am the last witness to creation. At least, that's how I've felt since I lost my sight. I can create the most marvelous images in my mind, invisible to the eyes of others. I inherited the work of creation; but sometimes the images come from a place so remote from my will that they're no longer properly mine. That's the way it is. There, in the depths of my "self," lurks the pit of the unknown; and I, once a scientist and a rationalist, have learned to be fearful of my own self. I dare not tread too close to that mysterious pit: for there, the projections overwhelm my imaginative capacities, laying me at the mercy of old*

*fears that I thought I had overcome many years ago, yet which remain
as potent as ever.*

My patient's name is Alejandro. He is a biologist. Three
years ago, he lost his sight. He began to vomit and to suffer
from headaches. His wife took him to a hospital where they
scanned his brain and found a cerebral tumor deep within. He
was operated on here in Mexico City. The scientific name for
his infirmity is both precise and sinister: "craniopharyngioma."
He has not worked since then. His wife cares for him tenderly,
but occasionally he feels totally dispirited. Surgery saved his life,
since the tumor would have increased the pressure within his
cranium to the point of causing death. But surgery did not cure
his infirmity definitively. This particular kind of tumor, with
its sinister name, will begin to grow again, slowly, and within
a few years it will become necessary to intervene a second time.
There is no way of predicting exactly when this will happen,
but it is bound to happen. Something unexpected, however, has
become critical to my patient's intimate, subjective world. Every
day, from dusk till dawn, Alejandro creates visual hallucinations
and plays with them.

"I see boats and old cars, planes and aerial battles. But I prefer
seeing rare fish, seahorses, and exotic birds," he tells me. Immediately my attention is drawn to the verb "to see" (which he
conjugates in the first person, "I see"), since my patient is in fact
blind, as blind as Jorge Luis Borges in his later years. "Before
becoming ill, I painted every now and then. In my adolescence
I took painting lessons; but above all I visited as many muse-
ums as I could: including those in Amsterdam, Belgium, Paris,
Madrid, Mexico City, Washington, D.C., and New York City.
When I wasn't reading biology books, I studied the history of
art. Some twenty years ago, I had the pleasure of visiting the

Vatican. Even now I can see that seignorial city, vividly, the Holy See, and revel in its architecture. I turn my attention to an altarpiece carved in wood, but then I feel a motion in my spirit: a tremendous temptation to make the altarpiece even more intricate, to make its form even more complex; and I work, carefully, at achieving this. With enormous effort I manage to gradually change the details of the altarpiece. I can re-create the entire structure of the Vatican with tiny imaginary sticks. Usually I can erect such three-dimensional structures in a matter of minutes, but sometimes I may need three or even four days to get it right."

JANUARY 13, 1999. This afternoon Alejandro speaks to me about his frustrations via the indirect language of parables, which is to say that I discern an unusual continuity between the tale he recounts and his daily experience.

"I like to interpret my dreams. I've dreamed, for example, that I am with my friends and we embark on an excursion in the woods. I get lost and arrive at a lake. I climb a tree to leap over the extensive body of water, but I find myself in an uncertain position. I've climbed so high as to be unable to climb down, but I can't continue climbing higher either because the branches aren't strong enough at that height. Then I direct my sight to the lake itself and peer into its depths: I see very large fish, primitive sharks, and manta rays. My own interpretation of the dream is that it represents my resentment against God for burdening me with an illness from which there is no exit. I can never be the man I was before, and only death would release me from this state, yet I do not wish to die. Sometimes, in the dream, I try to leap over the water, but I fall. I manage to surface, but the fish come rushing towards me and devours me.

Other times, I wake up, and yet I can still I see the creatures of my dream—the fish, the sharks, and the manta ray—floating in the air beside me, while I walk to the bathroom or the kitchen. This vision persists for more than an hour of wakefulness, beyond my control."

"Do you mean to say that once you are awake, the images of the dream continue to be present? How do you know that you are really awake then?" I ask him. "Pardon my ignorance, but when is it, precisely, that a blind man realizes he is no longer dreaming but awake? I mean, in my own case it's easy, since all I have to do is open my eyes and the early morning light tells me I'm awake."

"Give it some more thought, Doctor, and you'll see that you're speaking a little too lightly. Haven't you ever woken up at night, when the darkness is such that you might as well be blind? How, then, do you know you're awake rather than dreaming?"

"Well, in that case, I can tell by the contrast between the light within the dream itself and the abrupt shift to the darkness of my room in the middle of the night. There is always an abrupt shift of some kind. The shift might be from the quietness of the dream to the noisiness of the morning's activities, or the opposite—a nightmare may end when I open my eyes and ears to the stillness of the night."

"I agree, Doctor. There is always a shift of light or sound that comes with a change in consciousness. In my case, it's mostly a change of sound, but also one of visual images. In my dreams the entire space is full of lively, independent details. I would go as far as to say that in my dreams I find myself in a state of nature: though seen from the perspective of wakefulness, it is only the imaginary nature of the soul. In contrast to my dreams, when I wake up there is a sort of white, opaque background upon which I can design my own creations. The other difference is one of perception, wouldn't you say? Of course, you're the doctor . . . but speaking from experience, I believe that the greatest shift that occurs from sleep to wakefulness is one of perception. For example, I was telling you all about how certain images from my dreams, such as the sharks and manta rays, tend to follow me around after I wake up. Yet once I am awake I always know they are imaginary. Can you imagine what it's like to walk around your house, the kitchen, let's say, surrounded by floating fish? For a while it's amusing, sure, but if it lasts too long or if it interferes with my ability to concentrate on other tasks, it can become unbearable."

Alejandro seems dispirited. His hunched figure stiffens for a few moments such that I imagine he might break into sobs. I place my hand on his shoulder, gently, to let him know that I am there for him. His tears are stifled.

"I have so much to say, but no one wants to listen. Once I created a chess table with all its pieces, and I began to play. Very soon I lost control over the game because my memory proved insufficient to keep track of the myriad positions and successions of movements. Even if I could have managed to keep it all in my head, the game would have been frustrated, naturally, by the fact that I must play against myself. Who else could possibly join in such a game?"

JANUARY 14, 1999. Today I received an urgent call from the neuroscience unit. At midday, Alejandro was tranquil; then, suddenly, he began screaming for help. A nurse went to his aid. She found that his pulse was elevated, he was drenched with perspiration and was panting. He did not complain of any pain, yet he remained in a state of agitation, pleading for help. He was then transferred to the electrophysiology unit, where a record of his cerebral activity was effectuated so as to discard an epileptic crisis. The profile of his electrical activity turned out to be normal. By the time I met with him I found him more settled. He tried to laugh the matter off.

"I'm okay," he told me, "I just got a little scared by one of my visions."

"But you usually have control over them, isn't that right?"

"Almost always, with the exception of the most grotesque ones: worms, flies . . . they are beyond my control. I see the barrel of a gun. I take aim at them. But to no avail."

"Do your hallucinations appear suddenly or gradually?"

"It depends. When they're unwelcome, like flies and such, I see them in a sort of 'fast-forward' mode. But when I welcome their arrival, for example, when I'm constructing an edifice of some sort, I can keep the vision stationary for several hours."

"Is there any particular time of day when the more grotesque images appear?"

"Not really. It can be at any time. But the process is always the same. I feel nervous, desperate, an urge to shout or to flee, as if there were no air in the room and I were at the point of losing consciousness . . . at such times, I lose control over my visions. I see my grandmother on her deathbed, blood on her lips, just the way I remember her at the time of her death. I could still see perfectly in those days. Seeing my grandmother in such a fragile situation, so vulnerable, hurt me very much. I've never forgotten it. When those moments of terror come, the vision of my agonized grandmother appears with great vividness. I see that I am at her bedside in a large chamber within a hospital. I feel the urge to leave that place immediately. But I see that all around me there are hundreds of hospital beds, and in every bed I see my dying grandmother. Whenever my visions become uncontrollable, I take refuge in one of two options: the first is to force myself to sleep; the second involves casing or framing the nightmarish images as if putting them on stage or setting them on a theatrical dais, and next I invent some enormous curtains, and I gradually bring the scene to a close by drawing in the curtains, little by little. If I draw them in too quickly, the trick never works. But if I do it gradually and I try to relax, the nightmare of the hospital and the beds vanishes, slowly, behind the curtain. Occasionally this trick is of no use and no matter how slowly I draw in the curtains, my anguished grandmother remains there, suspended, incompletely vanished, and the whole scene begins to pulsate . . ."

"Perhaps the pulsating you describe corresponds to the beating of your heart?" I told him. In this fashion my patient and I develop a tentative theory to rationalize the nightmare. I take his pulse and teach him how to do it himself.

JANUARY 18, 1999. Alejandro is interned in the neurosurgery unit. He will never see daylight again. The optical nerves that transduce solar energy into the language of the brain have been destroyed. Clearly, Alejandro needs his inner light, the subjective illuminations that astonish and renew his consciousness every day in the form of hallucinations: flexible, moldable, often marvelous, sometimes terrifying.

I speak with my superior at the hospital about Alejandro's case. Impatiently, he refers me to journal articles on the usefulness of certain antipsychotics in suppressing hallucinations: "The Efficaciouness of Risperidone in the Control of Hallucinations," "The Efficaciousness of Haloperidole in the Control of Hallucinations," the exact titles do not matter: they all have the same disillusioning effect on me. I raise the matter with

Alejandro, but he considers the use of antipsychotics to suppress the images he creates daily to be an act of barbarism. I cannot help but agree, in this instance.

"I like religious and mythical images," he insists. "I'm an aficionado of Greek mythology; but I also create my own myths. I invent minor gods, having the ability to intervene in the affairs of men in real time. It's usually around twilight when I work on such projects. My palette consists mostly of greens and blues, and sometimes a flash of red. My inspiration comes from the turbulent incommensurable waters of the Aegean Sea, where I imagine two shipwrecked individuals on a raft. They are on the verge of perishing, condemned to solitude, isolation, hunger, dehydration: adrift on the depressingly vast body of salty water. Above them is the curved immensity of the celestial sphere from which my minor gods descend to save these souls with whom Poseidon couldn't be bothered."

I strain to summon the right words with which to confess to my superior that, in this case, I am compelled to disobey him, for I have not attempted to suppress Alejandro's hallucinations. His blindness has transformed him into both a wanderer through, and a guide to, the mysteries of creation. His hallucinations are the source of his prodigious creativity; but they can also be a curse. Fortunately, we have devised a treatment for his anxiety attacks. We conclude that if he can learn to maintain a modicum of control over the subjacent emotions in his visions, then he might he also gain control over their origins and, by extension, their very nature.

"Yesterday afternoon they came back, those terrible images of my dying grandmother. I remembered what we discussed, about the potential correlation between my hallucinations and the beating of my heart. So I took my pulse and I observed its rapidity. I became aware, as never before, of the palpitations of my heart, and its pulsations occupied the entire field of my consciousness: I saw an organ, yellow and red, bloody, pulsating so strongly it might explode at any moment. I feared that death was not far off. Just when I believed I had no alternative but to call for help or risk death, I saw my heart suspended in the middle of an empty, white sky. I took some deep breaths. Then the sky's hue took on a lighter shade of blue: and as my pulse began to slow and my respiration grew steady, I saw the light blue sky illuminated in the distance by the sunny resplendence of my heart. There were clouds in the sky, large puffy ones, which came toward me when I inhaled and moved away when I exhaled. Eventually only the clouds remained in the sky, swelling and contracting with the beating of my heart. The images of my agonized grandmother and my bloody heart completely vanished from the scene."

As I walk toward my superior's office, I think of that Russian story according to which a blind man returns to his home at night and in his hand he carries a lantern. "How stupid," someone tells him. "Why would you bother to cast light on your path if you cannot see?" The blind man responds that the lantern is not meant for him, rather for the people with functioning eyes to keep them from knocking into him or running him down. A part of me wishes that Alejandro might extend his stay with us, so that I might have the pleasure of learning more about his wondrous powers of creativity. I am blind to his creations, for only he can see them. My eyesight ends where the opaque backdrop of my blind patient's imagination begins.

Rebellion

QUETA NAVAGÓMEZ

Translated by REBECCA HUERTA

ℰℬ

People, the beach, the sea,
and the sun kept them apart. They found solace only at twilight
among the rocky crags where they could dream of a future
together. The man grew tired of this dream, however, ignoring
his heart and its longings. Now his indifference keeps them apart.

She observes him resting his head on the tanned breasts of a
woman with short hair and perfect thighs, a frolicsome woman,
fond of walking barefoot on the beach.

Rebelling against an arcane, obscure destiny, as eternal as
the sea, she climbs upon a jagged rock with difficulty to gaze

at the night sky, the tears in her eyes blurring her perception of the stars.

When the sun's radiant orb rises, it finds her still weeping. It ascends unhurriedly while her skin begins to dry up and her sight grows dim. Flocks of seagulls swoop down, picking at her limbs, but she does not so much as flail her arms.

As the sun reaches its zenith, crowds begin to gather, staring in astonishment at the exposed body of a mermaid languishing on a rocky crag.

Future Perfect

GERARDO SIFUENTES

Translated by CHRIS N. BROWN

ॐ

I EARN MY LIVING illustrating the future that men see. Scientists, engineers, and editors show plans and sketches of the machinery and landscapes their minds create so that I can translate them into a screen simulating life. This is a real job. My portfolio includes the most diverse futuramas: orbital factories, underwater cities, all sorts of flying vehicles and robots in action. The work is published in magazines, book covers, and video-game packaging. Some images are part of ambitious industrial projects waiting to be financed. Very few are realized, most because they are unaffordable, or the future inevitably defeats them, and in most cases it's better that it happened that way. The uncertain atmosphere of the day to come made me very pessimistic. In reality the future has no determined form, maybe not even a meaning, so one has to constantly reinvent it. Mr. Dobrunas agreed with me on this point. I met this character just when I had lost my confidence in my ability to create proper futures.

He showed up at the house one afternoon, referred to me by Professor Melampus, the futurologist from the university. Mr. Dobrunas presented himself like a doctor but never mentioned his specialty or the school where he studied. His tall figure in a tailored suit, aquiline face, and nervous temperament intimidated me. Coarsely overgrown eyebrows accentuated the obsessive and malicious look. Dobrunas needed illustrations for a biology project: the creation of a series of genetically altered plants whose details were specified in the beat-up binder he carried with him. When asked to elaborate upon his descriptions, since botany was a new theme for me, he appeared to ignore me and pointed at a Chinese communist propaganda poster hanging on the wall of my studio, in which a worker, a soldier, and a peasant looked confidently to the horizon. "This is the image of the world that I want," he said with histrionic solemnity.

My father, a popular political cartoonist in his time, told the story of a sixteenth century cartographer who marked the unknown sections of ocean incorporated in his works with chimerical monsters peeping out of the surface of the water. One day, the cartographer was surprised to hear of some sailors describing encounters with the creatures he had invented in the maps.

In Mr. Dobrunas' project, the plants with altered genes appear to be more the product of a delusional whimsy than the experimental fruit of scientific erudition. At the beginning his annotations described in extravagant detail sprouts of webbed leaves emerging timidly from thousands of test tubes in a greenhouse laboratory. But a few pages later, the flowers, and then vegetables, evolved to form part of a dark, unearthly garden, composed mostly of gigantic carnivorous plants with extravagant bulbs in every color. The doctor's spectral sketches were made with trembling lines reloaded with black ink. To read the notes, written with tiny, perfect handwriting, his digressions looked far from being scientific experiments worthy of being taken seriously. The findings focused more on a sort of metaphysics than genetic engineering. I thought about suggesting he first send the project to some specialist, but since the pay was good and immediate I decided to take the work. After that I dedicated myself to it. To give life to the improbable—the proposal wasn't for me to judge.

A couple of weeks passed. Dobrunas appeared to be pleased with the sketches I showed him on the computer screen, and confirmed it had brought to life this insane botany he had created with adolescent enthusiasm. Later he showed up with a briefcase stuffed with notebooks, in which he had written up a more ambitious plan than I had expected.

The schizophrenic paradise of Dr. Dobrunas included vast prairies seeded with gigantic husks, growing human fetuses inside like mandrake roots. This was the principle of an eccentric vegetable bestiary, in which he described a symbiotic society between humanity and the giant plants, and included the details of a religion created for the coexistence of the two species. As an exercise of the imagination it attracted me, if it could be done with the tone of a crude B-movie, with superfluous explanations to create these creatures. But what impressed me more were the conclusions: his proposal for an ambitious plan to repopulate the Earth. No more, no less. This wasn't a serious biology project, but a badly written space opera. I said so to Professor Melampus, but my mentor only urged my patience dealing with the matter.

One night, after finishing an illustration, I decided to put an end to the assignment. My mind couldn't continue. I re-read some strange notebooks, impatient and bothered—I envied that will to create universes. An idea started to germinate in my head. Ignore the restrictions of the futuramas and build the foundations of a story, just as if I were recalling a strange allegory of the living moment. My illustrations began to tell a fictional story. In it, a pair of scientists confront small armies of carnivorous plants and insects in a kind of chess match, the game board an elaborate Victorian garden. The story explores a day in which the men of science drink tea and watch the events play out through enormous magnifying glasses.

Within hours I found myself capsized into the creation of my own world. Soon new ideas surged forth, and I looked for the metapolis with its marginal life, the robots confused by the instructions of their masters, the abandoned space colonies. The future followed the plan of a map of an unstable world, and without question we needed to confront it or we would have no way to avoid being swallowed by the sea monsters.

Satisfied with myself, and after a couple of days inventing excuses for the deliverables, I decided to call Dobrunas and tell him project was cancelled. Contrary to what I expected, he didn't appear bothered and didn't ask for any explanation, and said he'd come by to get his material in a few days. Minutes later, in another telephone call, I learned the true identity of my client from Professor Melampus.

He was not a doctor. His real name was Igor Feréz, efficient clerk in a technical bookstore near the university. Dobrunas-Igor Feréz had unsuccessfully tried to gain admittance to the biology faculty, converting himself over time into an elegant autodidact, albeit with gaps in knowledge. His obsession drove him to sneak into classes and wander the campus carrying heavy books. The research regarding the plants was his opportunity to demonstrate his intellectual capacity to the world. Upon learning this, I had a mix of pity and scorn for him. Without a doubt, while we both imagined utopias, the essential difference was that Dobrunas firmly believed in them, whereas I just treated it like any other project in which I created variations on the dreams of other people. Igor's, while incoherent, was real in his mind.

After almost twenty-four hours of continuous work I had a few drinks and vainly contemplated the illustrations of plants and insects at war. I found myself so pleased with them that the furor of the alcohol made me elucidate new possibilities, some more interesting or absurd than others. The ideas of Dobrunas had provoked an enormous and anguished explosion of creativity in me that I could hardly control. The doorbell broke through hysterically. Opening the door I found Dobrunas, or Igor Feréz, who, in addition to coming to get his inseparable briefcase, held a black bag in the other hand. I didn't know what to say. In ordinary circumstances I would have asked him to come back the next day, but the alcohol had me in such a good mood that I let him in. His attitude was nervous indifference, like he was in a hurry, hardly thanking me for the work I had done up until then. He took out a wad of cash and offered it to me, staring raptly at the Chinese propaganda poster.

"I have something else for you," he said without looking away from the poster. He took a plant in a small flower pot out of the black bag. "Tomorrow I am going to another city."

The news took me by surprise. His gesture of courtesy moved me. But upon looking at the gift I froze. It was a carnivorous plant with the fangs closed, so small and delicate that I thought I would destroy it with my hands. I watched Igor Feréz's eyes, and on reflection invited him for a drink—at least I could get him to explain some things to me. Wary at first, he eventually accepted, with impulsive gratitude.

He explained to me the care the plant required, as well as his personal opinion on the latest advances in genetics and how they could be employed for the benefit of mankind. Apparently the dilettante was current with everything—perhaps he didn't miss a single popular science magazine or channel. I listened to him attentively, feeling a little dizzy from the drinks, and at some point in his talk I came to feel compassion for him. After all, nothing had to be stopped, even though it was a huge lie. He explained to me the origins of his plants: they were a species found in the desert that the botanists couldn't classify; he was lucky. Dobrunas had gotten ahold of a greenhouse to conserve some specimens, but he needed more funding to accelerate his research. The gift that he gave me that night was part of the first generation created by Igor Feréz.

"Moreover, they communicate with me telepathically," he said, "and tonight I realized what they were asking for—that maybe you could help me. Will you?"

As he spoke his tongue became a paste that prevented him from articulating coherent words. I only saw the small and inoffensive plant, as incapable of sending telepathic messages as I was to receive them. I decided that was enough and began to

politely get rid of him. I was feeling tired and no longer wanted
to continue playing his game. I pretended to believe him. I told
him maybe we could continue his plants project later. Dobrunas
got my message. He raised his head with dignity, got up on his
feet, made an exaggerated bow to say good-bye, and left with
a full glass of alcohol in his hand. He slammed the door on his
way out. To me this meant the incipient reign of the carnivorous
plants had come to an end.

My first professional project was to illustrate a petroleum-
drilling platform. That night I dreamed of it. I descended once
again in the bathysphere, and through a porthole I saw the
divers laying pipes. One of them, the one swimming without
equipment, was Igor Feréz.

I woke to a bug flying around my face. I felt raw, and sitting
at the edge of the bed I thought about putting the day in order.
I wanted to tell Professor Melampus about Igor's decision to
abandon the city. I got up to make coffee, but walking through
the studio toward the kitchen I knew something was going
wrong. An empty space on the wall revealed the absence of the
Chinese propaganda poster. I shouted angrily, surprised. The
lock on the door looked like it had been forced. Who but Igor
could be responsible for this theft? I was disturbed thinking how
this guy had broken into the house while I was sleeping. The
idea frightened me, since you could expect anything from him.
The little carnivorous plant was still on the table. I checked every
corner, making sure nothing was missing. His giant briefcase
was sticking out behind the sofa, like a chubby dog waiting for
its owner. He had forgotten it in his drunkenness, and I was
delighted about that. Without thinking about it too much I
emptied its contents. I found his notebooks, with his scrupulous

description of the planet he dreamed of constructing, along with a pair of classical music records, copies of the futuramas he had made, old science journals, and a beat-up manila envelope.

I was stupefied upon opening the envelope. The Polaroids inside showed adolescent girls dancing naked in a room, like fairies, each with a red handkerchief tied around her neck. There were at least six, and they looked very happy. I got excited, laughing morbidly. In another photo was Igor Feréz wearing a white robe. He appeared to be locked in an embrace with two of them. His face depicted a sinister grimace of certainty. Laughing with guffaws, I surprised myself. I decided to forget about the robbery, satisfied to know an intimate aspect of this guy, as interesting and eccentric as his world of carnivorous plants.

A week later five half-buried bodies were found in a greenhouse on the outskirts of the city. According to the news reports, all were covered in thick tangles while an army of insects feasted on them. They were young girls, with their necks cut.

It was a huge scandal. I immediately connected the news with Igor Feréz and called the police without equivocation. I asked myself what I could have done to help him when he made the proposal to me.

Thanks to Dr. Melampus I dug up other details. Of course the plant that Igor gave me that night, and others they found in his greenhouse, did not feed on human blood. That is a trait that belongs to a rare primeval species. A team of scientists headed by Melampus studied them in the hope of revealing their secrets. I never thought that these types of creatures had so much power of attraction. Now I found them fascinating. Their unconventional form, truly anomalous, is terrifying and perfect.

No one knows where to find Igor Feréz now. It's possible he went to the planet of the mandrakes, seeding the soil to grow giant pods and dance all night with the only nymph known to have escaped with him. People can see the faces of Igor and his dead girls on television programs, documentaries, articles, bootlegs, graffiti, and T-shirts. There are even a couple of very popular songs about the case. This is how he became part of the future. Only I could have illustrated it so well.

Luck Has Its Limits

BEATRIZ ESCALANTE

Translated by STEPHEN JACKSON

❧

"**W**E'RE LEAVING THIS pocket of turbulence," announces the pilot, while the stewardesses, swaying as they walk, place drinks on the tray tables of the most nervous passengers: among whom quite obviously is my husband. For the sixth time a uniformed arm is about to collide with my nose. The entire flight to Las Vegas was awful. I was even more reluctant to board the plane than I was to have my nose operated on. It was my husband who insisted on the operation and my husband who insisted on the trip. He knows that I am silently critical of him, which is why he downs his whisky in one gulp and quips, "I've stopped drinking, Jessica; see how I've stopped?" He went on, something about always trying to please me, but I tuned him out, trying to see the city lights. I love seeing cities from above, where they assume the dimensions of an architectural model, especially at night when they're all lit up, but my husband lowers the plastic curtain. Ever since I told him that I like seeing the city lights from above, he takes the window seat. "Are you happy, my dear?" he says with the arrogant tone of one whose business affairs have reached their zenith. He wants me to thank him again for the short trip. But I didn't want to come to Las Vegas. I would have preferred New York. "So you're happy, eh?" he insists with his hoarse voice. My lips respond with an utterance that keeps him quiet. Finally he shuts up, and the thought occurs to me involuntarily that Las Vegas might bring me good fortune. I imagine a city in which everyone is happy, where there is luck even for those who feel like I do, and I scan the pages of a magazine.

I know we're going to land, because he has already laid his chubby, sweaty hand on mine: our first contact for months, not including the "contact" that broke my nose and sent me to the plastic surgeon's operating room.

Our hotel is luxurious and modeled on Greek antiquity. I start up the hot tub, where I find salts, foams, and champagne. "Make it quick! We've got a dinner appointment with my partners!" says my husband. I obey.

In one of the hotel reception rooms we find ourselves among couples that mirror my husband and me: a rich old man with a flabby body puts his arm around the waist of a young woman endowed with slim proportions and a firm body. There is only one couple that clashes: one of the old men decided to bring along his ex-wife, a woman only six or seven years younger than he. He doesn't touch her. They walk separately.

"Ladies don't gamble, it's not elegant!" affirms one, the smoke from his Cuban cigar penetrating our silken gowns. One of the women says in an infantile and whimsical voice that men pay her to hear: "You boys go out now and win lots of money so we girls have something to spend!" Immediately, her fat patron rewards her, giving her a wad of one-hundred-dollar bills. My husband has no choice but to follow suit. I take the money from him and smile to myself, knowing that I should come back with no less than eighty percent of it and an explanation that I couldn't find anything worth buying.

The couples separate. The men go to the best casino. The women—commanded by Evelyn, the eldest and the one with the most experience in Las Vegas—go to a magic show. "Who wants to go shopping?" she asks, and, without waiting for them to answer, she waves her arm bedecked in jewels and cosmetics that cover her age spots. Accustomed to always having others decide their destiny for them, they all board the limousine without replying. Jessica is excited. She likes all things related to luck. She hopes that the magician will be a fortune-teller, one who reads Tarot cards, but at least initially it appears that he belongs to the lineage of illusionists. "All of you, observe this coin," he commands the public, "the price of happiness, as it disappears and reappears in the shape of your heart's desire." Jessica, who for the first time in a long time is interested in what is happening around her, thinks of the Tarot. She wishes to know her future, to know if there will be another man in her life, other trips. The magician's coin is transformed before the eyes of all into a deck of cards: and as luck would have it, it's the Tarot. It is all part of the act, of course, but Jessica insists on interpreting these events on a personal level. Her own thoughts caused the coin to reappear in the shape of the Tarot. She influenced the magician's will, and her assumption is reinforced by the fact that he approaches her table. Of course, he must approach all the tables; it's part of the show. But she doesn't know this or doesn't want to know it.

Jessica observes the ballerinas and remembers listlessly the time when she dreamed of being an actress in musical comedies. The stage lights change colors: the magician is going to bisect one of the plumed ballerinas. Smiling, the dancer climbs into a trunk. The magician opens and closes the hatches. All eyes are fixed on the young lady with the perfect body, not a single gram of fat or cellulite. Her curved and straight lines achieve such harmony that, at last, to the public's delight, she is destroyed. The saw has carved the young lady in two. Though everyone is familiar with this act, they applaud enthusiastically: especially Jessica, who imagined her husband in the trunk in place of the dancer, first whole then split apart. A dye the color and texture of blood responds to the magician's act of aggression. Some of the spectators grimace. The magician bows. The young lady reappears, repaired, while Jessica's husband, too, remains alive.

As they are leaving the show Evelyn abruptly remarks, "That was fantastic! Tomorrow we'll come back with the men." Jessica senses a small slip of paper in her closed hand and a glimmer of hope stirs within her. She can't remember how it came to be there, but she's certain of its significance. For the other women the magic show was interesting, even astonishing; for Jessica it was predestined. She knows that she will contact the magician, and she considers the favor she will ask of him.

The magician sleeps during the day. He dreams of his image appearing in the retina of a pair of formidable black eyes that gaze beseechingly. The number he wrote on that little slip of paper is dialed and his phone rings. He answers in Spanish because he still has not yet entirely woken up. Jessica thinks that this too is the work of destiny and she is happy, for her mastery of English is even more ludicrous than her mastery of her husband. "It's me," she says, and the magician understands. He imagines her in her bathrobe, pretending she is calling room service, while her proprietor soaks his fat body in the perfumed water of the bathtub. "Hurry up, Jessica!" demands her husband. The magician seizes the opportunity: "In the bar in the lobby of the Flamingos Hotel at noon." "Right, and don't forget the orange juice," she responds.

At noon the magician is no longer the magician. It's like meeting a movie star in a discount pharmacy. On the other hand, Jessica is as striking as always. She shines even brighter in the light: her slightly bronzed skin looks smoother; her straight black hair glistens from her bangs to her waist. Her charm is entirely natural, with the exception of her nose. She's had plastic surgery, thinks the magician, who always wanted to be with such a woman and who, despite his recent string of good luck, has only enjoyed such women as spectators or for brief encounters such as this one. The trouble is that magic, though verging on the supernatural, never really manages to transform lead into gold.

"That trick with the saw," she asks, faltering, "can it be modified?"

"What do you mean?" he asks, surprised that she would be curious about the technical aspects of the show.

She smiles nervously but stays silent. The magician encourages her:

"What sort of modification did you have in mind?" he replies, acting as if he were extremely interested.

Jessica expands on her question:

"Could it happen that the cut-up body doesn't come back together again?"

"What? Oh, sure, sure," he laughs. "That was done in France at the Grand Guignol."

"But did the person really die?"

"What person?"

"Well, anyone, really. I mean, is it possible that the individual might really die and no one would notice because they would think it was all part of the act?"

Their eyes meet. The magician's gaze captures each frame of her body's motion as she crosses her legs: her black high-heel shoe rises, traces a half circle around her shin and comes to rest about a foot from the bar floor. The magician's imagination takes over from there, recreating the same motion on his bed where Jessica sits nude, stripped even of her stockings, wearing only her high-heel shoes. He swallows his saliva.

"How long will you be in Las Vegas?" he says.

"Two days," she answers in a manner reminiscent of a princess in a fairy tale held hostage by a dragon.

When Jessica glances at her watch the magician is confirmed in his everlasting belief that he himself lacks attractiveness, that magic is the only magnet that attracts women to him, and he resorts to a trick. He takes out a deck of cards, allows her to check it for normalcy, and asks Jessica to pick one. She picks a Queen of Hearts and hides it under both hands. "Was it this one?" he asks her, spreading out the deck with consummate skill. All the cards have become the Queen of Hearts, to the delight of his audience. Jessica smiles and forgets her haste. For about twenty minutes the magician performs one trick after another and Jessica loses track of time. When he stops, she remembers that she has a husband and must go.

"I can change your destiny."

"Really?" she murmurs sweetly, "You'd really do that for me?"

"So long as you do something for me in exchange . . ."

Jessica flips back her hair. She imagines herself a widow, free, saved by a trunk, a saw, a pair of swords, and a beguiled magician . . . Well, at least it won't be as unbearable as doing it with my husband, she thinks as she and the magician ride the elevator to his room.

During sex none of his movements deserve to win a film contract, much less a prize. He is only thinking of himself. Jessica, however, is thinking of her husband. And for the first time, thinking of him makes her happy.

Back in their Greek-style hotel, Jessica's husband argues with the wives of his business partners.

"You just don't lose a person like you lose track of a package," he says furiously.

A bellhop hands him a wireless phone and, ill-humored, her husband takes it.

"Where are you? The other woman came back over half an hour ago . . . all right . . . all right, then!" he shouts. He presses the end button and orders a taxi to pick her up some three streets away from a shopping mall where, according to Jessica, she was waiting for the other women.

"She says she was window-shopping and you all left her behind."

None of the women contradict him, nor do they dare raise the subject amongst themselves.

It's nearly dawn. Some gamblers, clustered around a roulette table, hold their breath: her husband among them. He's bet twenty rectangular chips each worth five hundred dollars. His stubby reddish fingers rap on his gold lighter. I hope he loses. I hope they all lose. Damned luck: why does it always favor the rich? "Are you happy, Jessica? Your husband's a winner, sweetie," he'll say. I hate it when he calls me sweetie. Then he'll have to celebrate, of course. He's going to take me up to our room, where he'll want me to . . . but no, not this time: my luck hasn't run out entirely.

Jessica's husband has been losing at the roulette table for a while now, who knows how long? But he doesn't stop betting. He doesn't want luck to show up when he's not around to seize the opportunity. He keeps going on and on. His bet remains the same. But he won't be successful tonight. He realizes that when he has already left a merciless amount of money on the plush, green, felt-covered table. He's depressed. He hasn't even lost one percent of his wealth, but he can't stand losing. He turns to his spouse. "You've cost me more," he tells her resentfully. Jessica sighs.

Destiny, which according to Jessica rules all our lives, has led them precisely to the bar where the magician will perform. She prefers not to recall her pact with him. It was Evelyn who decided they should return. The magician is not there yet. When he finishes his show at the Fitzgeralds he will come here, sleep fifteen minutes in the dressing room, and then take his place two stories above the stage. He will observe Jessica with the very same group of Mexican women, and, of course, her husband will be seated beside her this time, flushed with whisky. "These shows seem to be getting worse every year, but for some reason they never go out of style," remarks Evelyn's ex-husband.

This time he will perform an escapist act in the great tradition of Houdini. A huge vertical aquarium in the center of the stage receives the magician who falls into the water, wrapped in chains, from the second story. He will have three minutes to free himself. Some people become distressed; others chat nonchalantly. "I've seen that trick a thousand times on television," says Evelyn's ex-husband, slurring his speech.

Another magician, a comedian, follows the escapist act and has the audience laughing. Jessica isn't paying attention. She is trying to guess how the magician will get her husband in the trunk—not because of his fatness, he already promised her he would resolve that difficulty, but because her husband is not the type to freely participate in a stage show. Maybe he'll hypnotize him, she thinks. She never for the slightest moment considers that the magician will not comply with his side of the bargain. She is convinced that her attractiveness will always cause men, in the end, to do what she wishes. When the magician (her magician) spins the empty trunk around for public inspection, Jessica is overjoyed. Her desires are perfectly fulfilled. The magician doesn't ask his assistant to get in the trunk, rather he requests a volunteer, while turning deliberately toward Jessica's table. The magician invites her husband, who waivers, but his wife insists, "You have to!" Emboldened by the whisky, Jessica's husband gets up on stage. The magician imagines himself at the Grand Guignol and exerts himself to the fullest, pulling strings capable of creating for an instant a fictitious reality that will fool the eyes of the beholders. All those present will swear to having seen the fat man get in the trunk and be cut in half. From the saw drips a liquid the color and texture of blood. Jessica, accustomed to others shaping her future for her, impatiently awaits the rising of the curtain. She feels nearly free, nearly in control of her destiny, when the magician (who belongs to the lineage of illusionists) snaps his fingers and restores her husband to life . . . to Jessica's life.

The Stone

DONAJÍ OLMEDO

Translated by EMILY EATON

For E.V.E.

☙

I CONSIDER MYSELF fortunate to contemplate you each day without the shadow of fear eclipsing your gaze: for, at last, you have found peace.

Today they came seeking answers again, Francisco foremost among them. I was worried for a while because several times he crossed the road, back and forth, walking pensively. Then he stopped a few minutes and fixed his gaze, questioningly, on the sculpture. I am sure he will return.

When you spoke to me of the contradictions inhabiting your heart, I could no longer find happiness, not even by watching the lovers shading themselves from the sun thanks to my shadow. From the time you turned ten until your final hour, this was your secret place to think, to read, and to dream. Time morphed the surroundings of this snail-like plaza, changing it into a gloomy place only visited to conceal some wrongdoing or to relieve adolescent passions. Ever faithful, you would come each afternoon to share with me your desires and annoyances. The blue tone of your eyes reflected your passage from innocence to maturity, of which I was the proud witness. The air of mystery contained in the ornamental comb in your hair was what attracted Francisco, whom I first met as a projection of your thoughts.

On the day it all began, suspicion, like a rumbling blizzard, shook my roots to the core. You arrived late to our meeting place. Accustomed to your light step, I did not recognize you at first. I observed with curiosity the whirlwind of a woman dressed like a zebra entering my territory. Your eyes revealed your identity. A maddening soliloquy reigned in the atmosphere. I tried to initiate a dialogue, but I quickly noticed that you were indisposed; pacing back and forth incessantly in the middle of the plaza, you were talking to someone whom I could not see.

Later, kneeling down, you cleared away the weeds and garbage with your hands. It seemed as if you were someone other than yourself. You did not stop until you had cleared away a semicircle in the middle of the snail-like plaza and your hands were bleeding. You were running away from something. On that occasion there were no good-byes. After that day I did not see your eyes again for three weeks. The plaza exuded sadness, and my melancholy scared away the birds, which preferred to abandon their fragile nests to fate.

You were limping upon your return. The ornamental comb no longer held back the messy hair on your head. We conversed, and you confessed that a strange force was taking hold of you: voices that insulted you, resounding in echoes, people who appeared in your bedroom, taunting you. In an effort to escape it all, you tumbled down the stairs of your house, injuring yourself. You lost your employment. At times you misunderstood Francisco. You suspected that he remained by your side out of pity; although his eyes revealed that he loved you. You imagined that you were, and always would be, a burden to anyone around you: a manic-depressive disaster.

I recall the precise moment when the solution crystallized in your mind. The sky absorbed the blue glow of your eyes. Your preparation was meticulous: a semicircle in the plaza was cleared away; seabirds adorned the grass close to the place destined for something special. On the day of your departure your eyes were flooded with tears. You wore the orange dress that so pleased Francisco, revealing your body's promises, and you embraced me, but the brilliance of your gaze was soon extinguished as the horizon announced the sunset.

The sculpture arose the next day in the semicircle. The woman's body was identical to yours, but two heads emerged from the torso, neither similar to yours. Others failed to perceive your presence in the statue. But I did. And so did Francisco. He drew near and stared attentively at you. He slowly extended his right arm to touch you with his hand, as he was accustomed to doing. Gradually, he too turned to stone.

This old oak tree that I am has learned much of human hearts.

Trompe-l'œil

MÓNICA LAVÍN

Translated by ANDREA ROSENBERG

For Charo

❧

She hadn't imagined, before getting on the bus, that a few jars of paint could have such an effect on her mood. She was excited as she returned from downtown and, pressing the bag of paintbrushes and acrylics against her body, slipped away to her room. Her daughter Lucrecia had asked her to paint headboards on the wall of the guestroom at the ranch during her visit.

"Dinner's at eight," she heard Lucrecia say.

Sitting on the edge of the bed, she took off her shoes and gazed through the window screen at the insistent green of the vegetation, which now, in the first shadows of evening, was spilling over with cricket songs and birdcalls in a choral effort to bring the day to a close. She didn't like the heat or the perspiration she felt all over. She wore her hair tied back in a tight bun at the nape of her neck. It wasn't a good look for her. Her eye makeup was smudging, too, a faded black rimming her eyes. She hadn't even dyed her hair before she left. She hadn't wanted to leave in the first place. She'd grown used to the sadness, the absence, to filling each day's movements and gestures with longing. It felt like a betrayal to try to distract herself from it.

She looked at the walls and took down the two watercolors of colonial street scenes that hung there. She moved them gingerly, terrified that a scorpion might be lurking between the painting and the wall. She'd tried using that as an excuse not to come: "I don't like trying to sleep and thinking there might be scorpions under the pillow, that they'll come up through the drains or out of the electrical sockets in the walls." But Lucrecia had insisted that everything was under control, and then deployed a powerful weapon: she said she needed help with the children.

The evening light stained the white wall orange. It was like a bare double headboard for the two beds, one of which she was occupying. She grabbed the hand towel and climbed on a chair to wipe the dust from the wall's surface. Dusk was falling. She would have liked to have excused herself from dinner and uncapped each little jar to play with the different hues. Forget the table and social niceties and have them bring her a sandwich—or not bring her anything, just a beer would do. Breakfast would come soon enough. But she didn't want them insisting that she'd get sick if she didn't eat. She didn't feel like explaining herself, wanted to savor her solitude.

So she sat back down on the edge of the bed, her eyes focused on that immense white space, an indifferent space, cold, oblivious to the way she was mentally distributing designs across its surface. She felt an urgency she hadn't felt in years, an agitation at starting a new project that in the past had enthralled her when creating set designs for university stage productions or when she designed a banquet for a group of lawyers (which at first she'd thought would be so boring) or when she'd helped a friend with a display for her shop windows.

She hardly tasted the guajillo-spiced enchiladas. She didn't eat much and drank some coffee, staving off the torpor of a full stomach being lulled to sleep by a fan. "Good night," she said abruptly and didn't stay to chat with her daughter after dinner the way she had the first few nights, when the room had filled with confidences, sorrows, shared memories, and her daughter's ineffectual consolations: "You look great," "You don't look at all your age," "There's so much still for you to do," "Enjoy yourself, go out with your friends."

She slid back the screen door to enter her room and then shut it again to keep out the swarm of mosquitoes that thronged beneath the hall light and would, if they discovered another light on inside, rush to loiter in its glow. She pulled the curtains closed on the melancholy gazes of the frogs who clung with sticky feet to the windowpane. Now shielded against reptile incursions and interruptions by family members, she put the lamp on a chair in the middle of the room, changed out of her linen blouse into a loose T-shirt, and started decorating the wall.

She began tracing the forms in charcoal. A great arch in the foreground, like an ogival window set in thick walls, on whose sill she sketched a bowl of fruit. In the background she drew the curving line of the horizon, which ended abruptly at a cliff with a solitary tree, its trunk twisted and rough. She didn't dare outline a square or rectangle to frame the image, because the arch itself was a window that extended the room and the only boundary should be the wall itself, which was simultaneously a window looking out on a different landscape and a wall enclosing the room.

She woke up late. Her daughter was already on her second cup of coffee and the children were darting around half-naked beside the sprinkler watering the yard. Her son-in-law was nowhere to be seen; he'd been out taking care of the ranch for hours. Lucrecia was worried about her: "Did you sleep all right? Is anything wrong?" But her mother's quiet expression and the appetite with which she consumed her scrambled eggs made it clear that she was in perfect health.

"You've started painting," her daughter guessed.

She spent the day looking at her grandchildren, accompanying Lucrecia to the market, watching the distant gray-blue river flow in the midday lethargy, while beer and conversation made the heat a little more bearable. She didn't talk much, observing another family's scenes as if she were attending a play. She waited for that dark hour to arrive that belonged to her alone. At lunchtime her son-in-law proclaimed her "much better, almost like before." Then she remembered. Like someone engrossed in a task who is brought abruptly back to reality by a sudden noise: her son-in-law's words reminded her of her forgotten mourning. She smiled in response. And Lucrecia explained, "It's because she's painting now."

He looked kindly at his mother-in-law, her hair undyed and sticky, her eyes shining.

"Can we see?"

"No, not yet."

That night she started on the color, tenuous hints of color: faint beige on the wall, dry green on the plain, a cindery sky above the horizon, palest ochre on the rinds of the oranges in the bowl. She stopped because the light of the lamp she was using to illuminate the painting made her eyes tired and irritated, and because, naked except for her T-shirt, she began to feel the cold of dawn on her bare legs.

Next morning, Lucrecia had left early for the market. A plate of fruit and a little cheese with bread and jam were waiting for her on the dining-room table. She reheated the coffee and ate alone, the silent flow of the river in the distance and red flowers scattered across the tender green of the flame trees. She contemplated that wild green, so unlike the green of her painting, which was parched and ancient, Mediterranean, like whitewashed walls and Valencia oranges. She hadn't willfully rejected the lush, unruly landscape of the jungle, but when she leaned out her painted window, her eyes surveyed a landscape that brought her peace, as if it belonged to her, as if at some point she had reclined on that windowsill before the simplicity of that landscape, with an olive tree as a witness and a bowl of fruit, lost in time, in any time at all.

She was grateful for the silence reigning in the house, for the fact that they were all gone, so she could take refuge in the landscape there in her room, through the arched window, unsettlingly close. At three in the afternoon, they tapped on the windowpane of the guestroom, summoning her to lunch, and seemed to have grown accustomed to her voluntary exile.

The maid took the opportunity to tidy the room and mopped hastily, trying not to stare at the wall, dizzy and disoriented, uncertain whether she was here or there. She whispered something to the cook, who sneaked in when everyone was eating to see what had so upset the maid. She, too, had to lean on the chair for support, while the room grew incomprehensibly large.

That afternoon, Lucrecia insisted she let her see the painting, said that if she didn't, she wasn't going to let her shut herself away anymore. Besides, she said, she'd commissioned the work herself and had a right to approve it. Her mother had no choice but to let her in. Lucrecia stood undaunted before the looming arch and the olive tree in the background. She felt the waxy rind of the oranges so close that she almost tried to pick up the one lying there on the sill and set it with the others in the bowl. The room had been transformed into another place altogether. It couldn't be called the guestroom anymore. Deeply moved, Lucrecia left.

The heat was brutal that night and the widow didn't go to dinner. The maid brought her a sandwich, a beer, and—Señora Lucrecia's orders—a thermos of hot coffee. Her hair damp with sweat and her sundress stained with moisture from her armpits to her waist, she undressed in a frenzy, eager to give the fruit bowl the whiteness that would transform it into porcelain and differentiate it from the powdery texture of the wall. Still dissatisfied, she placed a white lace napkin under the fruit bowl: porcelain on cloth, cloth on whitewash. Outside, the green and the old olive tree. Inside, the oily scent of orange rinds. Sweat trickled down her torso and seeped beneath the elastic band of her underwear to her pubis. She removed the last impediment and breathed deeply.

Near midday, Lucrecia slid open the screen door of her mother's room, opened the curtains wide, and called to her, apprehensive. Not a trace of her mother, except on the path to the olive tree.

Lions

BERNARDO FERNÁNDEZ

Translated by CHRIS N. BROWN

ॐ

Now we flee, hiding in the dark, moving away from the light of day. But it wasn't always so. There was a time when they were our plague.

The first lions appeared in the public parks. They always took refuge under the cover of darkness, hiding where the trees were thick enough and the grass grew tall enough to hide them.

Fleeing from us, they sensed that we were the ones responsible for the disappearance of their habitat, who took them into a captivity that quickly exceeded its capacity to house them.

At first we noticed the sudden decrease in stray dogs in the city. After a while, we started to see their gnawed bones scattered near the public gardens. As always, we didn't pay attention until it was too late.

If they had been an endangered species like gorillas, the panda bear or manatees, surely our zoos would have fought to have examples in their cages. But they had an overpopulation of lions.

And so they started throwing them out in the street.

The process went like this: in all the city zoos they gave the order to eliminate the excess lions, arguing that it's better to maintain fewer examples of a species so well-known and of such little interest to visitors.

There were dozens of cats sacrificed in order to keep budgets within reasonable limits.

That measure was quickly abandoned given the difficulty of eliminating a predator of such dimensions; the costs were almost the same as the original plan to save them, not taking into account the protests of the Sanitation Department, whose workers refused to dispose of cat corpses, nor the dumpster divers' rejection of the foul taste of lion meat.

But the orders were ignored, without discussion.

So that was how the first lions ended up with their claws in the streets, clandestinely removed in the middle of the night, near the public parks where at least they could leave their feces without being too obvious.

It's impossible to know precisely how many were left to their fate in this manner. The archives that contained the official numbers were destroyed when the political scandal broke. But the most conservative numbers estimate that there couldn't have been as many as the sensationalist media wanted us to believe.

The real problem is the high fertility rate of lions. A macho adult male has the ability to copulate up to five times in a single day.

Five copulations with five ejaculations included.

More than one was likely to be a success. This, without considering the absence of natural predators.

Although we ignored the parks where the early ones were released, now we know that at night they were emigrating to every green zone they could find, occupying all the available space bit by bit.

We didn't discover our new neighbors until much later. The morning joggers, unemployed old people, children, young couples, and drug dealers who populated the public gardens at all hours were observed by attentive amber eyes, whose owners hid under the shade of the trees.

The cats changed their habits, turning themselves into nocturnal beings. Dogs and rats were the principal component of their new diet. Food that, although modest, was never in short supply.

If it hadn't been for their showy dispositions, no one would have noticed anything unusual.

Until the famous incident of the lovers.

An anonymous couple went into one of the biggest parks of the city, looking for a cheaper intimacy among the trees than they could find in the hotels on the boulevard.

They say that they were so wrapped up in their making out that they didn't notice the policeman who snuck up on them quietly, trying to surprise them. The lawman's success was thwarted by an eight-hundred pound lioness who, stepping out of the shadows, charged before he could blow his whistle.

Terrified, the lovers fled half-naked.

The next day, the remains of the policeman and the clothes of the lovers were found in the middle of a big pile of blood.

The forensic investigators appeared at the scene of the crime , and determined without a doubt that they were dealing with a common workplace accident.

Two days later, in another park, a drunk woke up torn to pieces. And the next day a retired postal worker was mutilated: he lost his legs while taking a little nap.

It was the beginning of the attacks. Surely the authorities could have done something so that they wouldn't have found the others on the fourth day nibbling on a cadaver whose fingerprints (the ones that were left) matched those of a famous serial killer. This time the men in blue determined suicide and attributed the earlier deaths to him. Later they created a large file on the subject.

And so, perhaps urged on by the official indifference, the lions left their refuges to cynically strut their manes down our streets.

Without hunger, they are as tame as a little cat. But they eat all day, which is why it was impossible to know at which moment they would bite off the arm of a balloon salesman or swallow a kid.

Don't even mention their shit.

We tried to complain, to organize neighborhood committees that demanded the immediate elimination of the cats. But we only found deaf ears with the authorities, who felt that the more practical—and economical—solution was to avoid the public parks and cross the street if you saw yourself coming across a lion.

The media aired the news when it was of interest, but the

World Cup and the minor triumphs of the national team sent the lions into media silence.

And they would have been permanently forgotten if it hadn't been for the time during the tumultuous celebrations over a tie with the Bolivian national team when a horde of lions attacked the fans at the Angel of Independence.

They didn't wait for the statements of the government and the opposition, nor the television debates and the newspaper editorials.

In the middle of it all, the lions were settling into their new habitat. Soon they began to move into the big boulevards.

Crossing the street became a dangerous feat.

The advisors to the mayor, more preoccupied with placing their boss among the presidential candidates than coming up with a solution for the root of the problem, opted for an immediate treaty of limited scope and declared the entire city an ecological preserve dedicated to the preservation of lions, with the additional intention of controlling the population and adding a tourist attraction to the metropolis.

By then the cats had decided to occupy every green area they encountered; in no time private houses, schools, sports facilities and cemeteries were invaded by the city's new patrimony.

You could get up in the morning and discover that in the yard, whatever size it was, a family of lions had moved in, looking for breakfast. The occupants of the houses usually ended up being eaten.

Bones bigger than those of dogs and rats began to litter the streets, many with shreds of meat still attached. In little time swarms of flies became part of the urban landscape.

The rumors started to spread: that they attacked in packs,

that they were intelligent, that they were taking over the city, that there was no way to control them. The authorities denied it all, calling the media alarmists and asking the public to tolerate their new neighbors.

Until one day the cadaver of a child appeared.

The dawn broke, as if nothing, in the center of the Zócalo, at the base of the flagpole. This time, the city government couldn't deny anything because the news cameras got there first. It was an official provocation.

We were scared.

The mayor's aides decided that there could be opportunities to take a stand at the rear of the presidential palace, that they had to declare war with no quarter against the lions. And so that's what they did.

But it was already too late. There was no resulting program with which they could confront the plague. Firefighters, police and soldiers could accomplish little against the thousands of cats that lived in the streets.

One day a lion came into the center of the Zócalo and scornfully spit out the remains of a head. The skull turned out to belong to the mayor of the city. He had been attacked by a pride during an official ceremony in Alameda Central Park. The lions had been careful to leave it barely recognizable. Just enough.

And then the lion roared, as if proclaiming victory.

He didn't need to do it, by then they were already the landlords of the streets, of the parks, of the gardens, of everything.

Every day there are more of them and fewer of us. We have to take refuge in the shadows, while they sleep, now that they have gone back to being active during the day. We hide in the shadows, looking to steal some of their scraps to eat.

Sometimes the lions organize hunting parties to eliminate us.

Their nose guides them to our refuges. Sometimes we manage to evade them, but not always.

But where they hunt one man, another one turns up. Once they trap one another one appears.

We have decided to retake our city, even though we don't know how.

Now we are the plague.

A Pile of Bland Desserts

YUSSEL DARDÓN

Translated by OSVALDO DE LA TORRE

༺༝

TWO MELTING TABLESPOONS of butter in a saucepan at mid-flame resembled the process by which Lou had grown accustomed to being alone, respiring a sense of deficiency, sleeping on only half his bed at night. His dissipated condition was spread throughout his home with deliberate sluggishness—just the way that butter gradually turns from solid to liquid on the saucepan, eventually melting to the point of almost complete evaporation, leaving in ascendance thin columns of caramelized smoke.

Lou knew that sweetness replaces sadness. The mere honeyed

aroma of the desserts he prepared rescued him from the abyss, blending him with the universe as yet another ingredient seasoning the cosmos.

His wife's departure had shattered him. The tears and anguish that accompanied the consciousness of his loss drove him to prepare hundreds of desserts, one or two each day, all of them in hopes of her return. Yet since this did not occur, he threw them away, for when the aroma of a dessert vanishes, it no longer makes up for what is lost, becoming instead a simple, vulgar mix of flavors.

As he combined the sugar with the softened butter, Lou imagined his wife embracing him, sprinkling, in the midst of the desserts' fragrance, his face with kisses; as if it were all real, he saw her enraptured by each scintillating food particle, fusing with him into the Milky Way.

All for naught: neither the hundreds of aromas hovering about his kitchen nor the pieces of parchment paper infused with the smell of each dessert which Lou hung with religious care on the door could bring her back. None of the multiple aromas, no matter how exotic, were able to conjure her return. It made no difference how many times he prepared sponge cake with milk caramel, apple pudding, baked apples, mango mousse, Bavarian cream with soursop, imperial torte, or Peruvian blancmange: he was no closer to Alina.

Tossing in some lime and orange shavings, Lou cried as he dwelled on his feelings of abandonment, the bitter taste they left in his mouth—as if his teeth had been capped with in copper. When he closed his eyes, his wife's face appeared to him, a reminder that her absence was the very proof of his nothingness.

Lou didn't find it strange that, as he walked around, his body left behind a trail of bread crumbs, for he had been feeling frail for days. Sometimes, while sautéing fruit, he could actually sense his body crumbling; for instance, when he poured half a glass of orange juice onto the pan and a drop fell on his hand, he immediately felt his fingers softening and turning milky.

As the mixture on the stove thickened, he sat on the chair and observed the table. He saw his wife there, sitting and eating her French toast, as she had done each morning, humming a song and reading the newspaper. Reminiscing, Lou wondered why Alina did not want to have any children, and thought she must have felt embarrassed that he was a man who wanted nothing more in life than to be close to someone for whom to cook. He prepared every recipe and every dessert with her in mind, thinking of the smile she gave him on the day he told her he knew how to cook, of the mocking gesture Alina made when he said that ramen noodles is not real food, and of the intense gaze she gave to the veal in red sauce he prepared during their first week together.

As he thought of his life with her, a few warm caramelized tears rolled down his face, breaking minute crumbs off his skin. Lou observed the crumbs on his chest and brushed them off, as he did with the little milk curds dribbling from his lips.

Witnessing the bread rising up from his lungs, Lou got up and added to the mixture some slices of pineapple whose core he had cut out to avoid a harsh flavor. As he did so he felt alien to his house and understood that Alina's abandonment was meant to maintain a portion of sweetness in his life, the necessary amount to become in some way transcendent, even if it meant losing everything.

The pineapple slices would have to cook in the sauce for five minutes, enough time for Lou to open up a bottle of brandy and inhale its aroma. Brandy was not his favorite drink, but his wife had always thought it was one of the best ingredients one could use in the kitchen, and so he learned to incorporate it into his dishes, such as in the Romanoff strawberries he prepared on their wedding day. The memory of brandy and orange juice lingered on his palate, of Triple Sec and strawberries, of cream and sugar glass, resulting in his chest turning into an earthy crust of stale bread which crumbled onto the kitchen floor with each sigh.

Leaving behind a thin carpet of breadcrumbs, he warmed up a bit of brandy on the saucepan, stirring it every once in a while with a wooden spoon. The sweet fragrance of the fermented alcohol was delicious, like the scent of Alina's neck or like that of her hips as he followed the fragrant line to her thighs.

Fatally crumbling with each step, Lou grabbed a plate on which to serve the pineapples seasoned with butter and orange sauce, and added three tablespoons of brandy. He put the plate on the table, garnished it with mint leaf, cleaned the edges, and stepped away from the dish, which stood out from the kitchen's yellow walls, from the vapors trapped under the ceiling, and from the set of silverware he had bought on their third anniversary.

Lou sat on a chair, expecting Alina to appear through the door. His crumbling body left traces beside his plate. He closed his eyes, hoping to see her, hoping to tell her that he needed her, to share with her every dessert he had prepared and those that he had yet to imagine. Turning his back to the door, Lou heard the doorknob rotating and his wife pacing inside the house. He smiled while his moldy body cracked and fell to pieces, descending in a kind of orange-colored dust.

Alina entered the kitchen with the certainty of having seen Lou cooking, but all she found was his pineapple dessert, to which she drew near. The dust on the floor stirred when she pushed in her chair. Alina shook her head as she remembered their wedding day and their promise to be together forever. Yet forever is a very long time, she thought. As she tasted the pineapples for the first time, she felt the aroma ascend from her palate to her temples, inundating her with an incredible lusciousness. She sipped the sauce and felt as if she had been raised to the heavens and beyond. The brandy's perfume made her ecstatic. She breathed heavily as she felt the fresh pineapple glaze her throat with the most exquisite sweetness she had ever tasted. Alina, sighing between each bite, felt as if Lou caressed her through the dessert's sweet, creamy taste. She cried. After she was finished eating, feeling a quasi-celestial delight in her stomach, Alina wiped the corners of her mouth and remembered that she needed to distance herself from this place, to feel that she did not depend on anyone, that she was not bound by the flavor of a recipe, that, above all, she had yet to taste other flavors, to dip into other sauces, to simmer gently in the presence of another body. Standing up abruptly, she placed the petition for divorce on the table and left the house without glancing back. Inside the kitchen, the breeze tossed the breadcrumbs around, making them float like a starry shower, like crystals reflecting the light filtering through the curtains.

Amalgam

AMÉLIE OLAIZ

Translated by ARMANDO GARCÍA

⁊

IT WAS SAID that she was a
mermaid exiled by Neptune. She appeared on the island on a
Sunday, barefoot, wearing a thin dress, with a plastic bag in
one hand and a soda can in the other. It was the evening of the
carnival. She entered the muddled streets, observing the people
with her eyes the color of algae. She danced as if she were trying
on a pair of legs for the first time on the main square's dance floor.
Her movements reminded one of the swaying of aquatic plants
caught in underwater currents. Her scent spread with the breeze.

Fernando, the painter, picked up her scent and traced it to

the main square, where he beheld the dancing mermaid. At midnight, he carried her over his shoulder like a sack of oysters and took her to his seaside house.

Nobody came looking for Amaranta. The islanders swore that the sea owed her to Fernando. She, they said, replaced the love that Hurricane Gilberto had stolen from him.

In the beginning, the woman spent long hours by herself; sitting near the trunk of a palm tree, she hugged her legs as if she wanted to envelope her entire body. Her reddish hair cascaded mightily, savagely, in waves that almost completely covered her. Lost in prolonged silence, she appeared to have no voice. A month later, she was speaking to the plants, the sea, and Fernando: who sat beside her in the afternoons, caressing her with uncharacteristic gentleness. During the hours that Fernando prepared colors and canvases with white primer from Spain, attempting to capture her and the sea in his paintings, Amaranta swam in the nude: diving for such a long time that her thorax enlarged as if her ribs were giving way to larger lungs. She returned home wet, refreshed, and with the fish they roasted together at night.

When Fernando wanted to possess her, he gazed at her with nearly shut eyes, the slight expansion of his nostrils suggesting that he was guided by her scent. She slowly began to grow attached to him, like coral to a rock. Someone swore he had seen them frolicking in the sea or on the white sand. At dusk, they lit a bonfire on the beach. Fernando played the bongo and Amaranta danced until exhaustion laid them down under the heaven's starry vault.

Gradually, Amaranta began to amuse herself by decorating her body with colorful plastic bags, making strips from them and tying them together, wrapping them around her neck, legs, and arms like long, brilliant scarves. Resembling a bird with extended wings, she ran down the beach, playing with the wind.

Fernando found her one afternoon among the rocks, swollen and purple, unconscious, almost dead, the plastic strips that had decorated her neck now tangled on the rocks. When Amaranta recuperated, they cried tears of joy and embraced each other tenderly. After that, each morning Fernando and Amaranta set out together to walk along the beach. Fernando carried with him a fishnet over his should and a sharp stick. They returned home with the net full of garbage, leaving a trail behind them as they dragged it along the sand. Amaranta sat down under the crooked palm tree with her legs spread and with a fisherman's knife she cut the plastic waste into very thin strips. Then she struck the empty aluminum cans with a stick until they were reduced to strange forms with which Fernando made art. She whistled while engaged in these tasks: a faint whistle reminding one of the sound pelicans make before diving for fish.

Fernando abandoned traditional painting for an amalgam of painting and collage. Employing dyed sand, cans, and plastic strips, he designed shapes that resembled the ocean's depths: elastic pendants that moved with the breeze, cans that looked like rocks; his artworks seemed to emerge from a parallel dimension. Fernando sold the first, second, and third pieces at one of the island's hotels. He bought Amaranta sandals and dresses, a red coral necklace and ornaments for her hair. He bought himself a white guayabera, and he treated his wife to dinner at the hotel's restaurant. The guests greeted them warmly and watched them with curiosity. Amaranta appeared to them as a savage mermaid with shapely legs.

Fernando's fame surged with the tide. He received requests from other hotels and from private collectors. He added accessories to the cabin to make it more comfortable. He bought a finer hammock and pieces of furniture that he painted himself. There was still money left over.

The islanders began to hover about the artist and his lover. Strange people with cameras that had telescopic lenses also began to come around. Amaranta sensed their deceit and every day she spent more and more time in the sea.

Since everyone tells a different story, nobody knows exactly what happened. One morning, it seems, Fernando pounced upon the spectators, breaking cameras and dislocating jaws:

"You ran her away, damn you!"

They locked him in the town's jail until the bronze of his skin faded and his rage and tears dried up. Nobody ever saw Amaranta again. Fernando was released early on a Sunday morning and he went home. Taking his clothes off, he sat, facing the sea.

When a school of dolphins passed by the painter, Fernando leaped into the sea and swam after them. Some said that he became food for sharks, but nobody saw bloodstains nor did they find his remains, and most of the islanders were convinced that Amaranta had come back for him.

The *Nahual* Offering

CARMEN RIOJA

Translated by EMILY EATON

For Rodrigo Vilanova

❧

T HE EXISTENCE OF *nahuales* had always provoked fear and fascination in me. It astounded me to consider that the spirit of an animal could be at once my protector and my alter ego, especially when imagining the counterpart of the *tonal*, or physical body, as an entity with powers emanating from the dark side. It is also believed that a *nahual* is a sorcerer who can change into his or her animal spirit. Intuition tells me that the *nahual's* spirit is a savage and free being whose existence does not depend on its human complement, but I am careful not to underestimate its powers to transform my *tonal* into a luminous figure or to bend it toward its dark counterpart.

When I was a girl all this seemed an interesting and fascinating myth inherited from our ancestors. Altough I never felt close to these beliefs, than when listening to the legends and stories told by grandparents around the bonfire, when I started to dream about my *nahual* for countless nights in a row, however, fear sprouted within myself. Yet at the same time I was seduced by the prospect of discovering my own animal identity. This recurring dream featured a beast of enormous size: a masculine wildcat with black spots. Often in dreams I have seen him in such a threatening pose that sometimes it drove me to flee through the jungle's vegetation, and other times it paralyzed me with fear until I awoke from the dream drowning in inconsolable anguish. Last night, for the first time, I had the sensation of gazing deeply into his black eyes of sharpest obsidian. I lost all sense of time. I followed him, cautiously, immersed in a trance. We were in a sacred city, a labyrinth of ruins with infinite rooms, openings, and hallways. He guided me to the edge of the city, where a ravine separated us from a high hilltop. An old bridge led to the other side. Black shadows shifted over the terrain: the bodies of three *nahuales* crossing the crumbling bridge. The first was a coyote, the second a coon cat, and the third a vulture. They were followed by an Indian sorcerer who was carrying in his arms a wooden cross adorned with marigolds. Three dozen men, plus women, children, and a twisting spiral of smoke trailed behind the sorcerer. They were going to climb the hill in pilgrimage. The men went along singing and the women praying. Everyone carried translucent bottles of Coca-Cola from which to drink from time to time because the slope was steep. A few liters of rum were also in their possession. A boy shrouded in a cloud of incense carried in his hands the head of a young goat ready for the offer that would take place on the top of the hill among some eroded stone ruins. It had once been a temple, but nothing much was left of it. A very tall pole stood at the top of the hill upon which they fixed the cross and left offerings each year.

The offerings consisted of food, animals, herbs, incense, and flowers. But there was also music and after-dinner dancing around the cross. Still in the near side, on the outskirts of the city, I could distinguish a woman in a dark corner of the ruins: cooking alone, nearly in secret, intoxicating aromas enveloping her. She readied a large pot and filled it with a stew of meat, beans, and dried chilies. The pot bubbled on a stove fashioned from the cover of a metal drum container that had been stolen from a construction site. For fuel she used cardboard, rags, plastic, and wood scraps. The sorcerer ensured that the woman had that which she needed to cook in the fire.

They were celebrating the third of May, the biggest holiday of the year, marking the beginning of the rainy season and clement weather for the cornfields. Ironically, their generation no longer possessed cornfields. They dwelled on hard grayish terrain and resided in units of public housing situated along grids in infinite settlements spread out among the remote valleys and hills of the periphery of Mexico City. Because of the difficulty involved in crossing such a deep ravine, the only means of reaching the far side was by way of the bridge: and although the faithful had constructed the bridge less than a decade ago, it threatened to collapse at any moment. Nevertheless, they would cross it on their periodic pilgrimages because the Holy Cross had to be erected on the sacred site of the ruins. From the hilltop one could see a valley that had been populated, destroyed, and rebuilt so many times over that its rivers had dried up and its mountains had crumbled. The impression was that the end was near, disorder had reached intolerable levels, and complete annihilation might ensue at any moment. Nevertheless, new buildings were continuously being constructed over old ones, over ruins, over hollows. The men no longer raised crops in the valley. They had become laborers, and they constructed buildings by the hundreds, overseen by their foremen, who each year without fail permitted the laborers this one holiday: the third of May. After the rituals and the offerings, it would rain—a few days before or after—though for some years now the rainfall was acidic. It no longer fell on fields of corn or beans. It fell on the hard buildings and on the impermeable, grayish ground. The night before the third of May, day of the Holy Cross, the laborers would grow impatient waiting for the festival, the celebration, and the alcohol: but only those lucky enough to be employed were invited by their foremen. At one time almost everyone was employed, even if only on a part-time basis; but now the majority was unemployed. This woman cooked for the unemployed. She cooked for the duration of afternoon and evening, so the next day she would be able to feed forty unemployed laborers and their families who no longer had a foreman to invite them to the festivity of the Holy Cross. She always fed them provided that they participated in the prayers and helped carry the new cross and offerings to the hilltop. If they followed their *nahual* and pleased him in everything, they would surely have a good year. The difficulty was in knowing what the *nahuales* expected of them and in making contact with them, but this was the sorcerer's function. He would instruct the men regarding the specifics of the offerings, since none of them remembered the old rituals anymore. Curiously, the people no longer prayed for rain, rather they prayed that it would not rain: or else their neighborhood would flood again, garbage inundating the sewers, and many houses would collapse. It was expected that the population follow the *nahual's* advice: and they prayed to the ancient gods, to the comparatively new saints, and to anyone who might intercede on their behalf for employment and nourishment.

All afternoon the woman cooked the meat over the fire that burned thanks to scraps and pieces of wood taken from construction sites. The meat had a rancid odor. Newspapers strewn about the floor absorbed the blood from the meat. Working on the floor tired her out because her ample belly prevented her from sustaining a sitting position for very long. So she hung the rest of the meat from a rafter and tore it into strips from a standing position. As time passed her legs began to feel as if they were anchored to the ground and her ankles began to swell for she was a big woman with thick blood. There was a lot of meat for her to clean. The sorcerer hoped that with fewer workers, fewer guests, and so much meat, there would not be any quarreling at the feast. This year there would be no foremen present to defuse conflicts, none of the strongest laborers, none of the men who had taken jobs from others then refused to share their ration with the unemployed. The woman trusted the sorcerer to dispel envy, the evil eye, and foul moods, for the sorcerer had achieved mastery over his shadowy counterpart. She finally succumbed to deep drowsiness while sitting in front of the stove watching the pot simmer. It was almost twilight on a sultry day of the kind that anesthetizes your tongue and fingers. A radio playing reggaeton shook the silverware piled on a table. Bam, boom, bam, boom—the mugs and plates shook, and the bass was so resonant that even the dishes sounded like a leather drum,

a rhythm so primitive it seemed ancient, savage, accompanying the woman's slumber. Occasionally the fire sparkled with
fluorescent colors, greens or pinks, from the chemical makeup
of the burning scraps that served as firewood. The woman had
found herself staring fascinatedly at the magic contained in
the cauldron, the fire speaking to her, the voices of the *nahuales*
emerging from the dancing flames, when sleep overcame her.

The next day the evil eye would be dispelled because that is
what the festivals always accomplished, easing relations between
foremen and workers, and among the workers themselves. Of
course peace did not always reign during the festivities. When
food ran short, for example, someone or another was blamed and
a fight ensued that sometimes ended in blows and sometimes in
knives. When only some could eat and others went hungry, the
hungry ones would riot by nightfall, bursting into the homes
of those with provisions and attacking the inhabitants: taking
away the women and leaving the children crying and the men
nearly beaten to death. The woman had been staring at the
fire intently, and its hazy light carried her off, as the flight of a
vulture, to a luminous slumber. Her dreams offered her *nahual*
opportunities to heal her.

Doña Rosarito dreamed of a city aglow in white, built of a
substance more precious than gold. There was something secret in its construction. What made the city shine came from
inside it: intrinsic to the walls and the leaves on the trees. The
city shone with a light radiating from within the objects it
contained: a white metallic light, akin to silver or to the liquid
morning sun, flowing like sap through the veins of the walls.
There were pyramids with vertical staircases and thick walls
seemingly constructed not from stone but rather from a single
crystal rock of brightest amber. It was as if the temples were

made of golden plasma radiating light, an eternal light akin to the rays of the sun.

She dreamed of a very young girl named Huetzé whose skin was the same color of the golden city and her eyes of amber. Huetzé slept in the embrace of the leader of the community, a man with translucent eyes and smooth, cinnamon-colored skin. She dosed off as the sun was just setting and one could hear the laughter of many children who, after having sung and played beautiful instruments around a bonfire, had permission to run free among the trees, climbing them and caressing their leaves while their mothers prepared food and their fathers harvested seeds with the last light of day.

Huetzé's golden skin shivered. She pressed her breasts closer to the leader's body, entangling herself in his legs. She heard the murmur of children and felt the tepid evening breeze. The ritual drums sounded: bam, boom, bam, boom, and she dreamt that a peripheral tribe came and took away the women and children of her tribe to a hilltop. They set up a cross and were dancing around her to a primal rhythm. They drank liquor until they were growling and lurching. They ate meat until they were satiated. Afterward they quarreled, exchanged blows, unsheathed knives, and sacrificed the maidens in a bloody frenzy.

The meat was cooking very slowly on the burner, stewing in a sort of corn-flour gruel. Doña Rosarito awoke to the same flame with its sparkling green, pink, and violet phosphorescence caused by unidentified chemicals that were likely poisoning her lungs and confounding her mind. She thought of the privileged people who lived in the tall buildings her people constructed and kept their provisions chilled or frozen in tightly sealed chambers: abundant foods of all kinds, packaged in colored boxes, in plastic wrap, in aluminum foil. All that food would be enough to feed the workers' children for quite a while. The sorcerer informed the woman that this year the *nahuales* wanted the foremen to ensure that none of the opportunistic workers would be in attendance: that this year all the poor, the unemployed, and their families would eat. The stew contained the flesh of the opportunistic workers and the foremen. When the pilgrims arrived at the hilltop, they set up the cross and made an offering of the victims' flesh and blood. The three *nahuales* ate only corn and did not linger but returned across the bridge. Rosarito recalled the golden city of light from her dream where there was fruit for the children, quality seeds with which to feed the elders, and where mothers would gather happily around a bonfire to share their food.

Huetzé awoke too. Her nightmare was unpleasant. She remembered havin seen a sorcerer carrying baby-goat heads at the foot of a cross and an obese woman dismembering human bodies, placing them in chunks in a large pot. But Huetzé had found her *nahual*, a powerful jaguar that led her from the jungle vegetation to the hilltop. She had glimpsed the future and remained frightened even now by that nightmare in which humanity constructed one cube box upon another.

Huetzé shook herself from her slumber and hugged the leader, waking him with a kiss. It began to rain. It was time to go down and help carry the grain that had been harvested that day. It was time to protect the bundles of food in straw nests fastened to tree trunks from the rain. From those nests our community would eat for a year. Afterward it would be time to rest, to smell the wet earth, to tuck in the children, to listen to the wise elders. It would be time for song and melodic music by the bonfire.

Pachuca Second Street

LUCÍA ABDÓ

Translated by EMILY EATON

To Lucía, my daughter

⁊

Do the streets have a name so that one doesn't forget
where to find them? Or is it so that one doesn't
stumble onto an anonymous slab of concrete?

—MILOSH MILOSOVIK

T HE STREET is semi-deserted;
it's time to start my homework, no excuses. I take my notes out
of my notebook, Venus at four o'clock; lights from a siren escort
the Breathalyzer at one. Fortuitous sex, permitted and furtive:
between one and three; baby's bottle at five, hungry child at four
fifty-five. The city pretends not to rest, I have provided it with
a pacemaker so I can monitor the variations of its rhythm and
prevent it from catching up with me. It comes close, destructive,
looking like a melodic Sisyphus insistent upon tying my hands.
Like daybreak, some lyrical event crushes the shadows and exudes

a feeling of complexity. Adrenaline diverts me, moves me. I look for the siren at one, what does the time matter? The important thing is not to dream. Green, red, white: rigid helmet, shades of the Mexican flag; my damned obsession with understanding the language of others. Remember to abandon them once and for all, you must perceive them, they have dismantled your segments, just like that, one by one, purposively, no excuses. Where shall I go? To the end of the rainbow, next to the pot of gold, gay pride, or a spectrum of light made visible by the rain splicing it? What does it matter, the important thing is to dream. The moon runs—by the time I leave, it won't be dawn yet; luminous events are closely and directly related to understanding, the greater the solar light, the lesser the drive to dream. The brightness makes it even more impossible to hide myself. It dawns: Baudelaire's wings flutter away; I don't want to lose you. Something wet falls down my cheeks. I don't know whether to name it, my senses weaken with structured language; better to sing it, better to feel it, to penetrate it and let it penetrate me. I offer the possibility of a brief instant of eternity. The women dress in white, the men in gray, the androgynous ones run loose awaiting the final judgment; and I am just trying to put my pieces together, that's it, plain and simple: like an unfinished symphony, unknown, insignificant, which in its flight yearns to burst with air.

The fat ones are in mourning, a big fat man outside of the Treasury Department. Damned mania for considering myself insulated . . . the economy invests in me. Milk, cereal, water, eggs, meat: your flesh . . . ode to the infinite. To touch you is to touch myself without losing my mind. Is this lust? It depends. Excitement, in my case: for others, perhaps a kind of excessive thirst more proper to whores and clerics. Although, isn't there something clerical about my flight? Night approaches and my notebook traces its last notes; it discovers that it is surrounded by monsters and coffee-shop fortune-tellers; it's resting on Nemesis, at the feet of Bacchus and Venus, with an amnesiac tranquility that disrupts sleep, abandoning it to oblivion. Women, men: common sense? The boy from apartment 602 is crying. Not long ago he returned from Paris. His mother takes him to the park.

Wittgenstein's Umbrella

ÓSCAR DE LA BORBOLLA

Translated by SARA GILMORE

⁊ᴓ

Seeing as people either meet each other or they don't—and may fall in love or not as a consequence—suppose the rain compels you, a man, to seek shelter under an umbrella held by a woman. You ask her, "May I?" and she, hesitant and surprised, weighing the pros and cons, says "No," that it's her umbrella, and that you should go. Suppose you listen to her and head off in another direction, stepping around puddles for one block, two blocks, three blocks, until you find an awning under which to take cover, and there, right there, a killer is waiting, and it is written that he's your killer, and when he threatens to take your wallet or your life, you tell him to take your life because you're wet and cold and you don't feel like living anymore; though it would be nice to have a cup of really hot coffee, and since there are no coffee shops around, he sticks you with a huge knife and from the ground you see him take off with your watch and your wallet through the curtain of rain from behind which the girl emerges, the same one who didn't want to shelter you under her umbrella; and as she walks by, you die.

Suppose heaven exists and you decide to die at six in the evening or rather that your killer takes your life at that exact time, or better yet that time itself—which coordinates everything—precisely synchronizes all the clocks so that you die in your country at six in the evening without you or your killer having to worry about being late. If heaven exists, you'd arrive at its gates about quarter after six, towed by the vapors of a smokestack located not far from the place where you'd left your body. The gates are opened wide, you go in, walk around, look this way and that, but there's nothing there, you don't find anyone. Heaven is an infinite hangar, you think, and an image passes through your mind of the woman who refused you the dry shadow of her umbrella in the midst of the rain.

Suppose that in addition to heaven existing, God exists; your ascent and arrival are as previously described, only now you find a counter and, behind the counter, a caretaker in a green frock coat who signals with his gas lantern for you to come closer. You take a few steps and, in doing so, surmise from the tacky green glow of his frock coat that heaven isn't the place for you, that you should concern yourself with other matters, like deciphering for certain the reasons why the woman refused to share her umbrella with you, and so on.

Suppose God exists and He's waiting for you, that you

traverse eternity and infinity, which is nothing more than an endless series of little waiting rooms, waiting rooms and ante-rooms, and at the end, or what you consider to be the end, there's some furniture resembling that of a café, some comfortable blue vinyl chairs made of imitation leather, and you take a seat convinced that if God awaits you then you must be meeting Him here. Your fingers rub the chair's blue upholstery, as if to confirm its reality, and out of habit you want to order a milk shake: but God, even though He's waiting for you, never comes; and in His place, mixed up with your longing for a milk shake, comes the memory of the woman in the rain who told you, "No."

Suppose God does make an appearance: this scenario might be identical to the last, except that if God indeed shows up, the color of the caretaker's frock coat would have to be a bishop's purple. You're sitting in the blue vinyl chair craving a milk shake and right then God arrives dressed as a waiter, wearing a bow tie and a hairnet over His head, and on a tray He's carrying just the milk shake you wanted. You respectfully get up and invite Him to have a seat. God complies and you offer Him a sip of your shake, but He refuses, explaining that He's just finished eating, that He appreciates the offer but isn't in the mood. You draw back, a little embarrassed since you realize that the confident way you offered him a sip was probably inappropriate, and, afraid of having acted so rashly, you ask if smoking's allowed. He says that it is and even requests one of your cigarettes. Your hands shake, as it's not easy to light a match in the face of God. But God inhales and says, "Great cigarette; is it of blonde tobacco?" "No," you answer without realizing that you're correcting God Himself, "it's of dark tobacco." "Not as processed, right?" He asks, and you say "Yes," that they're cheaper. "Well, it's great," He repeats. You inhale the smoke and think that they're really not very good but you don't dare say it. God looks around and says something about the blue vinyl on the chairs, something about how it looks like leather. You agree. God finishes his cigarette and says: "Well, I've got to go now, it's been a pleasure." You aren't able to say anything, and, as God moves away between the chairs that look like they're upholstered in blue leather, you remember the way your killer moved down the street while it rained and the face of the woman who refused you shelter under her umbrella.

Suppose now that there's no afterlife. You die at six in the evening because the rain forced you to look for shelter elsewhere and beneath the welcoming awning that seemed harmless was hiding the criminal that would kill you as a result of the woman who refused to share her umbrella. The smokestack releases dirty puffs, the rain slices through the smoke, carrying it down to the ground as soot, a sodden fine powder that the water sweeps into the gutter along with your last breath. Next day your rain-washed body would be found, "A dead body!" they'd shout, but you wouldn't hear anything, not even the sound of the rain or your killer's footsteps, or the "No" of the woman who excluded you from her umbrella, you wouldn't hear or see or know anything—no milk shake, no small talk with God, no caretakers in frock coats, no chairs that looked like they were made of leather. There would be nothing.

Suppose, alternatively, that you seek shelter under her umbrella and she says, "Sure, walk with me," and you're hesitant and surprised, since you've suffered the consequences of her prior refusal. You begin to tell her that the "No" she gave in another story delivered you into the hands of a killer, which led to some small talk with God and a series of bizarre scenarios, at which she laughs, just as you and she walk past the door where the killer lurks, soaking wet, fated to kill you. Since the weather is so lousy and it's only six in the evening, she suggests that you go to a café on the next block which, of course, has blue vinyl chairs. You enter together, shaking the raindrops from your clothes. She orders a milk shake and you order coffee.

Mannequin

ESTHER M. GARCIA

Translated by CHRIS N. BROWN

જ

A man looks at the mannequin
desires its face and its body
doesn't matter that its mind is empty
he just wants to possess it.

He buys the mannequin
loves her entire body
covers her in flowers, in kisses
and from his mouth come vipers
that joyfully enter
the ear of the doll.

Now the mannequin wakes up hearing him,
the doll turns into a woman
to endure semen,
venom,
in her mouth;
to endure the wounds
in her synthetic skin.

The man gets fed up with her presence
treats her like a slum whore,
the mannequin cries wax tears,
the man mocks her as she leaves.

The poor mannequin rests now
in the dumpster,
her silicon heart
is disassembled inside;
those ancient kisses,
of that guy,
are now
taking apart the body.

Mr. Strogoff

GUILLERMO SAMPERIO

Translated by STEVE VÁSQUEZ DOLPH

ↄ৮

...**a**ND THE LOCALS SWORE
that the man in the black gabardine was certainly Mr. Strogoff,
resurrected after his butchers—twins who looked more alike
than if Mr. Strogoff had gazed in the mirror and seen his own
reflection—stabbed him for seducing one of their wives; and
they swore that his butchers intentionally produced something
like fifty wounds all over his body, and that blood gushed out
in spurts from several spots, especially his nose and mouth;
and one of the butchers swore on the Cross of San Jacinto that
blood was oozing even from his eyes and that he drew his last

breath in the biggest pool of purple blood he had ever seen in his entire career of slaughtering, adding that it was likely that not a single drop of plasma was left in the man's body, which ended up yellowish, its open eyes gazing at nothing; but neither of his butchers supposed the man in the black gabardine, Mr. Strogoff, would reappear, safe and sound, as though all he had received were pricks from acupuncture needles one night at the break of dawn, and that he would suddenly hypnotize the fatter butcher with a pendulum, paralyzing him head to toe, but leaving his sight intact and seducing his redheaded wife again, having his way with her half the morning until the wife herself would cut the butcher's throat with a long, very sharp knife that Mr. Strogoff had given her, decapitating her husband in one stroke, whose head bounced several times on the floorboards, rolled across the room and tumbled down the stairs, while the wife packed a bag with her belongings to flee with the man in the black gabardine, Mr. Strogoff, and now she is not only his lover but she assists him in the strange laboratory that he has run for decades; and so the locals spread the story of the reappearance of the man in the black gabardine and the dreadful news reached the other butcher, who swore to avenge his twin and kill Mr. Strogoff again even if it cost him his life, and that he would do it as many times as necessary, since it was obvious that Mr. Strogoff maintained sinister connections with the unfathomable forces of the underworld that resurrected him each time he died or that his mode of survival was attributable *ad libitum* to the spells and potions he manufactured in his laboratory where he did not permit entry to any of the butchers; furthermore, the butcher made these proclamations to the locals in a voice that shook deep down, either out of anger or fear, for that same day the butcher had heard that the man in the black gabardine, Mr. Strogoff, had lived in the neighborhood since before their great-great-great grandparent's time, or maybe there were a multiplicity of Strogoffs, and the butcher thought of this when he glimpsed a shadow move amidst the shadows behind him, feeling suddenly and inexplicably trapped by the most intense horror he had ever felt, at which point it occurred to the butcher to frighten him off with a fire, and he started piling up chairs, a table, a chest, his mattress, anything flammable that he could find, adding even some newspapers in a strategic manner, and when he heard Mr. Strogoff's steps, so familiar to him, trying to force their way past the door, he took out his old gas lighter, sparked it and lit the pile of objects guarding the entrance; the man in the black gabardine could still be heard for a while trying to force the lock, but when the blaze grew big enough the butcher calmed down and he heard Mr. Strogoff's steps receding from the entryway; meanwhile, the flames reached the next room, the curtains and even the pendulum clock, that tall piece of furniture his mother bequeathed to him, and when it was no longer possible to read the time on the clock's face because of all the smoke the butcher realized that he had no way of escaping the fire; after hesitating a long time, he hurled himself toward the core of the blaze, that is, toward the entrance to the house, hoping to break the door down with a thrust of his shoulder, but the door did not budge and as the flames reached the butcher's body he dropped and crawled toward his bedroom, seeking refuge in the bathroom; lying on the floor next to the bedroom door, he put out the flames on his body and tried to roll under the bed, but the locals found him next to the door, charred, his arms extended as though an individual who also disappeared in the blaze had dragged him there by the shoes; after the firemen put out the fire, which had spread to neighboring houses, some of the locals claimed that next to the newsstand on the corner stood the man in the black gabardine, Mr. Strogoff, with the redheaded woman: and that, together, they suddenly disappeared . . .

The Mediator

ANA GLORIA ÁLVAREZ PEDRAJO

Translated by ANISIA RODRÍGUEZ

ॐ

Iₙ ᴛʜᴇ ᴛᴏᴡɴ of San Sebastián Bernal situated in the Christian state of Querétaro, we are all very devout. From the first to the fifth of May we hold festivities in honor of the Holy Cross, which is celebrated at the peak of a rocky outcrop. Although it is a three-hundred-fifty-meter climb over steep terrain, it is well worth it. At that height, it's as though we are close to the hand of God . . . our prayers are the ones He hears and answers because they are practically whispered in His ear. Generally, I pray for the poor souls in purgatory. Their cries during the night are not bothersome to hear, but their exile is what saddens me. Nobody should be neither alive nor dead; without a destiny, poor souls anchored to the earth by their sins.

On bended knees I move forward until they bleed.

I resort to Saint Marta, Saint Úrsula, and Saint Teresita to intercede before God the Father for the poor souls in purgatory. I know His heart is softened because I have clearly seen how many of them have been raised up to the light. Those who are left are content to follow me back into town. I cannot always guess their intentions, for at times they have saved me from dangers along the way but on other occasions they have attempted to kill me by pushing me against rocks. I don't hold it against them because I know they act out of desperation. Their efforts are all accounted for and they will be assigned a place in Heaven or Hell, ceasing to be drifting spirits tormented by uncertainty.

Finally arriving at home, I am grieved to find their darkened cloudy eyes beyond the window pane, staring at me resentfully, as if to condemn my useless prayers. In the end, just like them, I am nothing but a sinner, just as forsaken and just as estranged from the world. Perhaps this is why each day, little by little, I distance myself from life and listen more intently to the beckoning voices of the dead.

The Pin

LEO MENDOZA

Translated by ARMANDO GARCÍA

و&

A WOMAN ON THE subway wore the pin. It was different from the other ones he had seen. It wasn't inviting him to lose weight or open up a bank account. Its design wasn't flashy or bold. The pin was plain white and so big that it almost entirely covered the lapel of the individual's tailor-made suit; however, it bore a message so small that it was nearly impossible to read. He read it out of curiosity or mere habit, for he customarily read pocket-sized illustrated novels starring cowboys, or those designed for truck drivers, and sports newspapers, quite rudely, over the shoulders of his fellow travelers.

The message on the pin aroused his curiosity because the question it was inviting him to ask was peculiar. He had seen dozens of pins in his lifetime but had never paused to reflect much on them. Those offers to lose weight or to invest one's money seemed to him a waste of time, especially given his station in life, always in a hurry, rushing to meetings from one edge of the city to the other.

It was the simplicity of the request that attracted his attention: "Ask me about happiness." The pin's bearer didn't look particularly happy. When she sensed the man's gaze her expression was neither warm nor welcoming, rather she turned around with a hint of fear in her eyes. Despite his best efforts, the man had fallen for the message. He had known happiness as a provincial child of humble origins, but destiny had ruined his chances at holding on to it, seizing him from that paradise and dragging him to the city where he had become what he was—a senior medical-supplies representative: successful thanks to his scores of clients from the four corners of the city, successful thanks to his selfishness, successful thanks to his capacity to crush anyone attempting to overshadow his company's business. In fact his public-speaking skills and proud demeanor made him the logical choice when, some six months ago, the chief of staff had to be replaced. He utilized his newfound seniority to court the biggest clients in the company's portfolio from every neighborhood in the city.

His teammates spoke ill of him. They called him a miser because at those bar parties masquerading as meetings (which he rarely attended) he never left a tip: and because, despite his success, he preferred to travel by bus or subway. His lack of generosity offended his colleagues, whom he treated as potential rivals and from whom he jealously guarded the secrets he had learned in his twenty years on the job. The rookie salesmen viewed him with admiration and envy, yet he felt even more threatened by them than the veterans.

His inner dissatisfaction hidden by his outward success prompted him to follow the woman with the pin, pressing his way through the sea of bodies crowded into the subway car, mostly lower-middle-class travelers who despised his vain appearance and the company identification card displayed ostentatiously on the upper jacket pocket of his tailored suit. When he came just within reach of her shoulder and she seemed as though she were about to turn around, the door of the orange subway car opened and its human cargo lurched onto the platform, sweeping the woman with the pin away with the tide.

That morning didn't go well. Four appointments, none of which produced good results: only promises, vague remarks, and further appointments. He attributed his failure to the bad luck of running into the woman with the pin. He ate at the same restaurant where he had always eaten for the past five years. The food was cheap, it tasted good, and he rarely left a tip, justifying his stinginess by persuading himself that it was more of a cafeteria than a restaurant. Even so, the waiter, a pleasant elderly man with a slow pace, went out of his way to serve him and even patiently tolerated his scolding if the bread or utensils weren't present or if the fruit juices on the menu were bland. Lunch revived him. Three appointments awaited him that afternoon, after which he would return to the comfort of his home to watch the news, always consoled by learning of the misfortunes of others, even murders, so distant from his life that they could be erased with the push of a button on the remote control and a good night's rest.

He treated himself to a silent pep talk about how his fortune would improve after lunch, but, when he realized he had lingered too long, he made a dash for the exit, hardly noticing the lady with whom he nearly collided at the door. While digesting his meal in that fleeting subway trip which took him from Colonia Moctezuma to Observatorio, the image of the pin suddenly flashed back from the depths of his memory before vanishing once again. The rattle of the subway drained out this fleeting association, and his thoughts wandered to more pressing matters.

His afternoon mirrored his morning. He ended up arguing with a secretary who banished him forever because he had refused to give her a paperweight with the company's logo. It was one of those rare occasions when he found forced flattery and all such courtesies necessary for his job unbearable—and he simply exploded. But he also knew through experience that the misunderstanding would be resolved upon his next visit, when with feigned remorse bearing no correspondence to his true feelings, he would present her with the acrylic figure, and she, before allowing him to pass, would make a sardonic remark followed by a smile and forgiveness. This was a ritual he knew very well since he had married one such receptionist: the kind with fulsome, curly hair and tight-fitting skirts. His marriage ended six months later because she, as he so bluntly put it, didn't measure up to him.

But he did not consider that a defeat. It was barely a bump on the road. Not for nothing was he responsible for the training of the company's new employees, a task which he performed meticulously, having read all sorts of personal self-help books and expert guides on superior management practices. He knew what he wanted and—even better—how to get it. If success meant bringing down a colleague, especially one who interfered with his ambitions, he wouldn't hesitate. In fact he had rid himself of several such individuals. Two or three of those whose agenda differed from his had fallen prey to his wiles. He was thinking of this and of his future with the company, when again he spotted the woman with the pin among the sea of people in transit.

The woman with the pin avoided him as if deliberately refusing to clarify his doubts, slipping through the crowd awaiting the train; but the man was more agile and caught her up just as the subway's doors were opening before them. He reached for her shoulder with the firm intention of questioning her about the riddle of the pin. A human tide rushed over them, heaving them into the depths of the subway car and scattering them in opposite directions, but he held firm.

The person with the pin no longer was a woman but a man; moreover, a man bearing a striking resemblance to the chief of staff the pursuer had replaced just six months ago. By all accounts the former chief of staff, though physically distinct from his younger replacement, had been akin to him in spirit, ambition, egoism, and the persecution of his subordinates. Yet one day he mysteriously relinquished his post. His replacement proved to be so successful that within a few weeks on the job he had purchased a new car, leaving it parked near the subway station and using the subway to move between appointments because it was cheaper and faster.

According to what the new chief of staff had heard about his predecessor, he wasn't the type to wear a pin on his lapel reading "Ask me about happiness." Yet the resemblance between his predecessor and the man with the pin was undeniable. The younger man got off at the same stop as the man with the pin and tried again to reach him. Yet once again the man with the pin sought refuge in the crowd. The younger man (proud of his good physical condition, the product of regular use of his gym membership) was faster and managed to grasp the other's shoulder just as the doors opened to another train. There were so many things about happiness that he wanted to ask him.

Future Nereid

GABRIELA DAMIÁN MIRAVETE

Translated by MICHAEL J. DELUCA

ℰ

To Óscar Luviano

 Y ou can't precisely say the
moment when you started to look for him, when you repeated
his name in a low voice or where you were the first time the
preoccupied brush of your hand at the nape of your neck warned
you that you love him.

You can, nevertheless, remember when you knew he inhabited the world—just like you—and the image comes to you
luminous and long, a golden cord someone uncoils to you in the
abyss. You remember you'll call at the door and Ricardo will let

you in, everyone will be drinking beer, but you didn't feel like it. You drank a glass of sparkling water with crushed mint while you listened to the cheerful drumroll of the party. Someone will toss out a question—the lost genealogy of a Greek hero—and another urged you to respond, a formality you resolved truthfully and with humility.

"How do you know so much, Nerissa?"

"This girl reads everything, even cereal boxes. Ask her anything," and each happy phrase from this horde of witless clowns will make you yearn more for the quiet company of books. Ricardo warned you, and on the pretext of needing your help, he'll take you from their circle, bringing you to a closet stuffed with papers, books, and relics. In this tiny room you finally felt comfortable. You'll observe your friend's foreign hands arranging, dusting, cataloging pieces and pages on one of his little portable devices. You thought of all those people who live perpetually in the process of moving, until in some remote place, without any traces of their past life, they encounter peace. But you weren't born in the wrong place, rather in the wrong time—so how will you be able to find your place without any possibility of moving?

"Choose something to borrow for the week," the kind voice of Ricardo will offer, a compensation for the evening's embarrassment. You asked for a book with green edging and silvered letters. You'll nurse it among the rush of bags and carts on the metro; you scrutinized the index, eyelashes knitted for your astigmatism, and will choose page 23: "Umbrarium" is the name of the story. You found it very moving. You noticed the initials that hid the author's name: P.M. You descended from the car and return to your house feeling that you inhabit the world of the story, the air transformed by its pages into a terrible, kind sorrow enveloping your breast.

("Umbrarium", page 26.)

It's not that I, in the natural passage of my life, have
never encountered a virtuous woman. On the contrary,
I have admired the strength of friends and the beauty of
passersby; I have contemplated at length their gestures,
I have laughed along with their voices full of ingenu-
ity; modesty will not impede me from recording that
I've loved the sensations of their shapes and warmth.
Nevertheless, no one before had ever submerged me in
the depths of Agape like she did, the Nereid . . .

You'll love the Nereid, not only for the similarity of her name
to your own, but for the water that carries the word and the
creature. More than once, you'll read over certain passages in
the bathtub, walking in the shallow end of the pool where you
work out, or at that table by the fountain to which you escape
at mealtimes. You'll return the book with regret. You wondered
whether it wasn't one of those books that must be stolen, and
you considered saying to Ricardo, "Give it to me. It isn't yours
anymore, please." But sense will return to your head, and like
the good girl you'll be, you returned it. And like the good girl
you are, you'll ask in a timid voice in each of the libraries on that
street—the one that right here is called Montealegre—if they
have anywhere the story of the umbrarium. Wide-eyed you'll
describe the green cover, the silver lettering . . . but nothing.

How many of the small hours of morning did you spend thinking of his words spun like crystals, or bells, or silken flowers?

("Umbrarium", page 28.)

Worn out like the stone of the cliffs against which the
cruelest waves come, at last I made the hard passage

between one love and another. I was fed up with
feeling like an outsider, undervalued for manifesting
towards women (maidens, widows, or children) a respect that has never been common in the men of my
time. While my contemporaries thought of women
like mares or furniture, a part of their patrimonial
inventory, I wished for a companion I could talk to
about all this in tones of grand indignation, someone
I could converse with as an equal, ache to be near all
the time, hoping for some future scene together . . .

Later you'll get up in the middle of the night with insomnia, feeling stupid for not having tried a data search already.
On a first look, you'll think you've only found the covers of
intangible, discontinued books. But on immersing yourself a
bit further, you discovered a trail of knowledgeable informants,
your breath drawing you closer and closer to the screen. You'll
uncover the name and a brief biography: Pascal Marsias, a peculiar personality in the cultural life of the country during the
nineteenth century, born in the same city as you. An author of
scant, late-ripening productivity, whose principal themes are
love and fantasy, voyages of time and space. His work consists
of a few stories published in newspapers, the magazines of the
era, some anthologies (the one you'd already read stood out as
the most recent), and a book of poems: *Songs for a Future Nereid.*
Then he disappeared, no one knows how or when.

As if this shock isn't enough, your cursor encounters the
button to display images, and you'll click with trepidation.
Immediately, a photograph. You could feel the blood beating
in the veins of your wrists when the image filled the display: a
charcoal drawing that showed a man like any other, but in his

face, you saw his words reverberate; his lips, in which it would require only the merest impulse to find delirium, evoked in you a tremendous familiarity. You'll wonder if what you perceive is an echo of something that can't yet be said; if the future can't, sometimes, be impatient, showing itself imprudently in the moment. You rejected the idea immediately, thinking yourself crazy.

In your belly something will shrivel at the thought of the unfortunate distance which sometimes separates us from souls so attuned with our own.

("Umbrarium", page 31.)
The feeling became more urgent when I reviewed my travelogues. Paradoxically, I was already incapable of controlling my will, but this only made me desire more to find her. I dedicated myself to completing her, to sketching her out on paper like a character in one of my stories: what would please her, how she would move, what kind of friends would surround her. Under which horizon would she live? A distant one, as it turned out, utterly remote, like my subsequent trips, but nevertheless, that night, in the umbrarium, for a moment I could make out her face . . .

You adored the writing of Pascal Marsias for many reasons. But above all you'll say you loved that compassionate vision, the humane discourse that lay within the story. That which seemed the story of a haughty man, so desperate at not finding a worthy wife that—like Pygmalion—he decides to construct her himself, was in reality a grand apologia of love, reinforced by his last lines:

I thought it useless to create the Nereid. If something like her could be forged, it was the world that would make it possible. Since then, I carry out my part, trying to be a good man who delivers unto others the virtue lodged within him.

A great love—an inheritance the world deserves, you thought. You'd like to underline the words in this book as a substitute for a choir of caresses.

The next day you'll call in; you said, "I'm not coming. Nothing's wrong, it's just that I feel the flu coming on and I don't want to get anyone sick." The metro will be the cradle of your desire, the rocking of a yearning that made pleasurable your most ordinary gestures. The air from the open window will lift the black threads of your hair to your mouth, dampen them with your saliva, something close to a kiss; and the wind, a strange gust, will toss some woman's clutched papers into the tunnel. You picked them up, because you're kind.

Downtown is boiling beneath each step you take because of that obsession of yours with covering your feet, though springtime has already announced itself with violets and yellows. You took notice of the clear sky; you were inspired by the freshness of the March air, feeling around you the serene embrace of the present. You'll travel all the shelves, entering, leaving disheveled and blushing from the street—whose name has changed—a maiden on Don's Street, one volume, another, another, dampness, dust, sawdust, ink, leather, buttery paper, your weak fingers pulling at your lower lip, and you'll say, "Could you please look for anything else by this author?" and your coral-colored mouth outlined peaches in the air when you pronounced his name. But nobody had it. You began to despair, until, turning a hot, white corner, you saw this little bookstore, the owner just removing its padlock, opening its rusted shutters. You'll walk up to her without hesitation, giving a gasp of amazement on discovering that the tiny door leads to towering walls closed off by massive bookcases, books like a fortunate plague. You'll search among labels affixed with transparent tape, feeling the pulse of the words crawl up your arm. You didn't want to ask for help, finding him yourself was the reward. And you did: two shelves away the book waited in solitary anticipation: *Songs for a Future Nereid.* Trembling, you'll pay with a translucent bill; they'll take their time giving you the change, but you didn't open the cloth cover. You'll want to keep hoping—for what? You won't be able to decide, but that's how you preferred it You'll feel a wave of gratitude because you felt that this moment was marked, as if someone had put a silver bookmark between two pages. You'll know it was that moment which brought you here.

"Nerissa!" You heard the flutter of your name in the street, that dear, familiar voice, and you spin around . . . Ricardo, who has already shouted at you several times, and you ignored him. "Do you know Pascal Marsias?" you ask him desperately.

"I don't think so." You looked at him with sorrow. And omitting what you had to omit, you'll tell Ricardo about him.

> The Distaff of the Golden Cord (page 10)
> The fates' thread wastes no metal.
> I discovered it last night,
> in the umbrarium
> made of aromas,
> of shirts turned inside out.
> Generous thread of time, traveler
> your destiny is Life, future or past
> I saw in that false laudanum dream

what Dante's delirium never envisioned
not the vast inferno
but my secret desires
with their entrails exposed
the solitude of that familiar house
—at midnight, the candle and I—
my young sex in the lake, the trees
I saw my father . . .

You'll realize the intent of the poem. You read somewhere that it was "speculative fiction in verse," but in its presence, its unraveled seams, its scent—an eternal scent of lime and dusty perfume—you knew immediately that it was a recipe, a set of instructions. For some reason you remembered those old books of witchcraft ("legs of a spider, dragon's tail"), a set of precise instructions, though with uncertain results.

In this way you'll know there were tailors who after buttoning their shirts backward were able to drink tea in their childhood homes, and women who while folding socks witnessed the revival of an empire. As usual, you were afraid of confusing life with a book, and the mere possibility that all these things might come true tightened your chest. "Is this true?" you'll ask yourself, with the naivete of someone who's never read a lie, your hand pressed to your brow. You'll blend in the air his name and a hollow sigh. You looked in the mirror, yearning for it to be him looking back. You laughed at the idea, just so that you wouldn't feel completely crazy.

You arrived at the last group of verses. The delicate down at the nape of your neck will stand on end in a feline gesture; a shiver ran through your body a few lines ahead. In the last poem, you'll find what you were searching for:

Song for a Future Nereid (page 42)
Sorrowful notion,
I wanted to see what was to come;
in this blind faith of mine for the future
I saw the ashen destiny of my house
porcelain stained by banquets of mud.
I saw Montealegre street crowded with small trains,
lights all incomprehensible.
And I saw you.
returning nereid, close and Apollonian
I saw you moving
inhabiting the air with goodness and grace
You carried in your body something I had lost
Light clear as jewels caught in your hair
Somebody called you Nerissa

(Nerissa, like you, like that afternoon, and the street, and Ricardo.)

and in the simple consonance of your name
I understood it was you I had lost and recovered.
Return, future nereid
find out our plot
its invisible trail of scents and sundials.
Walk without fear
for one thing is certain:
the umbrarium already awaits the hour
when it will harbor us again.

You thought of burning the book like they burned books
of sorcery in the old days; unsettled, struggling between panic

and wonder, you'll crawl into a corner of the bed. There can't be any doubt: it's you.

Either the book was telling you about yourself, or you're mad. What blessed blindness will make you decide for the former?

Half-dressed you'll arrive at Ricardo's; he'll say, "I'm glad you're here, though the hour is a little odd."

You took out the book, inventing stupid excuses: "I have a report to write, due tomorrow, and I need this book to finish it."

Where to go? Which station do all these impossible trains leave from? You're well accustomed to stories where there's a giant machine with calendars and levers and buttons that don't make any sense. But you'll be astute: you've noticed that such stories always have less science and more sorcery. You'll resolve that the place where the witches are safest is in your own house, and you returned to this refuge, soliciting companionship from a stray cat, just in case.

You'll review again and again the pages of the volumes written by Pascal Marsias, the touchscreen tarnishing with the sleek marks of your fingers; you'll search again and again each class of formulas (botanical, mathematical, mechanical) for going back in time: none is useful for bringing him to you. You'll touch the sensitive outline of your lips, knowing you're loved across some kind of interval. You wept for the cruel condition of your love, your human insignificance. And at that moment, true gratitude, a true sympathy with all the variety of life took form in your bones, your flesh, your scent. And it was then that followed a victory for all lovers: you got up, brushed away tears on the way to the desk where rested your notebook and plume, and you'll begin to inscribe:

Dancers have the code in the movement of their bodies, birds in magnetizing the air with their beaks. Me?

It's not only a question of knowing the method. To discover it, one must know who one is. Who are you, Nerissa?

In your mind there arrived in a mob the answers given over centuries, in pages and pages, but which will cost you only one of your own.

Who am I?

On the paper the ink began to flow like thick, black blood. Brilliantly and definitively you'll write:

> I am Nerissa. I swim and I read. I believe in the impossible worlds imagined by people, in the tacit truth of books, the life of the stories. With greater strength I believe it now that I feel myself a part of a story. I am Nerissa, I am the future nereid. And Pascal Marsias made possible the world necessary for me to live. I write these lines in order for the words and my body to shape the precise machine . . .

Here you'll stop, as with the corner of your eye you perceived some movement. You didn't notice when all the shadows of the world shifted to the opposite side, but the tingling in your belly made you continue.

> I want to reach for him, towards the only moment I hope for. I know it's possible because I've already succeeded, in some skein of the time his travels have made . . .

Your mirror will reflect other walls, other light; you sighted immense folios and a roof woven with vines that release sweet, earthy odors; you avoided movement for fear of undoing what you'd done . . .

because he, Pascal Marsias, has seen me in the umbrarium.

And as the vertigo of Time throws you into its abyssal current, I, Pascal Marsias, leave to one side the quill and the manuscript of your story, for I see you appear in front of me, beloved Nerissa, here, in the umbrarium.

"Future Nereid" recounts the love of Nerissa for a forgotten, eccentric author who studies forms of travel through time. It is a story of books and characters generated, in their time, by other books and characters. The first is Henri de Campion, who lived in France in the seventeenth century and of whom Michel Tournier wrote in *The Flight of the Vampire,* producing a man outside of time deeply lamenting the death of his little girl. The second is Els Bri, a character from the story "Quality and Strength" by the Gallician Xosé Luis Méndez Ferrín. Els is an invention of the Eastern writer Seida Sokoara who manages to regain life several centuries after his death. So in reality, it could be said that "Future Nereid" is a love letter to these books and their authors.

GABRIELA DAMIÁN MIRAVETE

Pink Lemonade

LILIANA V. BLUM

Translated by TOSHIYA KAMEI

To Ramón Mier

ঌ৵

Hunger is a powerful organizer of the conscience.

—MARGARET ATWOOD, *The Year of the Flood*

SHE WOULD BE woken by any sound, however faint. But before the footsteps began, a light flashed briefly in the darkness of the warehouse. She opened her eyes, tightened her muscles, and brought her hand to her chest. Lately, she had to keep quiet. Her life was now a silent movie. The colors had also faded, literally and figuratively. Everything was rubble, bones, rust, and pain. Avellaneda crawled out of the plastic barrel where she slept covered with *ixtle* sacks. She appeared from behind shelves filled with bottles of herbicide. She saw him there.

Agitated, a man looked around him, trying to adjust his eyes to the semidarkness. Suddenly, he whirled as though being attacked from behind. Realizing he was alone, he sighed with relief. Just like her, he was dirty, famished, and fearful. There weren't many civilian survivors. Whether you were armed or not made a huge difference when you fought for the last remaining food. A little more than a month ago, mobs finished looting all the supermarkets and convenience stores. Because of eco-terrorism, farm production completely ceased, but, while food reserves lasted, life went on with the illusion that the crops would grow again and everything would go back to normal.

Farmers, including those who took part in uprisings and massacres against transnational transgenic producers, soon realized that normal seeds couldn't survive plagues and droughts. Food production plunged. It provided barely enough for them and their families, but nothing more. Faced with food shortages, the governments of the developed world set aside all the grains for human consumption and the livestock pastures for sowing, and cows, chickens, and pigs had to be sacrificed. Food became a luxury that only a few could afford. Some pundits called this phenomenon the "Somalization" of the Western world.

The man stopped near the shelves under a faint ray of light coming through a small window in the upper part of the warehouse. Now she could get a better look at him. He wasn't so old, in his twenties, but his beard grew wildly and his skin was badly sunburned. He wore a military cap that covered his black hair, except for a few tangles. For a second, Avellaneda remembered the portrait of Camilo Cienfuegos in her best friend's house. She had cried for all her family and all the people gone. In some cases, she saw their dead bodies. In others, as weeks turned into months, she became certain of their fate. Even so, remembering the portrait of the Cuban revolutionary and her friend made her eyes teary.

Maybe she moaned when she cried, or he felt her eyes upon him. The man suddenly turned and saw her. Avellaneda couldn't guess what he was feeling. His face didn't turn red, but rather pale. Even though she was the one who was frightened, the man took out his knife and held it in front of him. Avellaneda noticed a slight tremble in his badly scarred arm. She barely managed to raise her hands to show him that she wasn't a threat.

"I'm not armed."

"Come out and show yourself," he ordered firmly but gently.

He patted her down and then slipped the knife back into its sheath, made of a thick fabric. Avellaneda turned her head toward the shelves. He followed her. If he was going to kill her, he would've already done it, she thought. It wasn't a good idea to stay in the open part of the warehouse. For a long time no one had come in, but the streets were now more dangerous than ever. With food production halted, the world economy came to a halt. Money was useless without food to purchase. Force was the only law. After looting, pets and stray animals were the first targets. Of course, wild animals were fair game for those with guns and hunting expertise. In coastal cities, the sea was still full of life, but starving city dwellers lacked fishery technology and organization, and they ended up destroying boats and fishing equipment. What followed was cannibalism and subsistence farming, always threatened by thieves.

Avellaneda led him past behind the shelves to a part of the warehouse filled with herbicide tanks. One of them, lying horizontally, was the one she used to sleep in and keep an eye on the main entrance. They sat on upside-down buckets. The floor was strewn with cardboard pieces and wrapping material. They remained silent for a while, staring at each other awkwardly, like a couple of patients in a dentist's waiting room.

"I'm José. José Durruti." He extended his hand toward Avellaneda, but she didn't notice it, staring down at her own shoes, which were too large for her. They belonged to a stranger lying dead on the sidewalk. She removed them from the dead woman before her body disappeared. The shoes had high heels, broken ones, tortuous for walking.

"I'm Avellaneda," she finally said, and looked him in the eye to show him she wasn't afraid. But she was actually shaking inside her overalls that she found in the warehouse and were now her daily outfit. She wore anything underneath but always covered herself with the overalls the workers used in the warehouse when everything had been normal. Her secretary dress was now a small lump that doubled as a pillow inside the tank where she slept. Durruti. The man looked familiar to her. She straightened her back and wrung her hands. "Are you hungry, Durruti?"

Asking that question under the circumstances was unforgivable. It was obvious. Everyone was hungry. But it was also a courtesy of the past, an anachronistic kindness. José Durruti nodded, trying to hide his desperation, and she said she could offer him something if he waited there. She had her back turned toward him while she removed cardboard pieces and cans that hid a small metal door. Another chance to kill her if he wanted to do it. But when she turned back around, he was still there, like Monterroso's dinosaur. The difference was that he was one of the terrorists who had started it all. She was sure, not just from his last name, which wasn't very common, but also from his burnt hand, a large reddish white scar that she pretended not to notice. When the authorities were searching for him, using all the mass media, they always mentioned that particular mark:

a homemade bomb had exploded and left him scarred when he was a teenager and began to make explosives and put them in ATMs. Avellaneda sat on her bucket again and handed him a plastic container filled with dog pellets.

He thanked her with a nod and began to gobble. She gave him a bottle of the rainwater that she had caught from the flat roof. While she watched him wolf down the dog food, she told him that the warehouse belonged to a company that sold things for farming and livestock, Monsanto, Dow, etc. She said the company names slowly, trying to see Durruti's reaction. After all, wasn't he one of the terrorists who had destroyed the labs, factories, and headquarters of the large transnational corporations? Wasn't he the one who torched the CEOs? At least that was what the papers said, when they were still in circulation. But Durruti's face didn't change. He kept eating, stopping only for sips of water. The she asked:

"Who are you?"

"I told you already."

"You don't seem like him," said Avellabeda, taking a few pellets herself. Some were round and others bone-shaped. She was always careful to ration her meals, for when her stash of dog food ran out, she would have to leave her hideout and behave like the others. So far she had survived on food for cats, tilapias, pigs, chickens, shrimps, dogs, and cats. Perhaps she shouldn't have shared her scarce resources with a terrorist.

"You forget who you are when you're alone for a long time." He struck his chest a few times, trying to swallow. "Is this all you've got to drink? It's horrible."

Avellaneda remained silent, without chewing, like a daughter-in-law who forces a smile when her mother-in-law makes one of her uncouth remarks. She thought about a bottle of pink lemonade she had kept since everything began. It was a new brand that used real pink lemons, genetically engineered using blood oranges and other fruits. "No artificial colors, same taste," the label said. The ads were geared toward feminine women dressed in pastel colors of the eighties of the last century. Many times Avellaneda had been tempted to drink it, but, after ogling it for a long time, she decided to save the bottle, as if it were a sort of assurance that she would survive until the next morning. She felt that sharp pain that ripped through her spine every time someone burst into the warehouse, while she crouched down, holding saliva in her mouth, praying her heartbeat wouldn't betray her. But he roared with laughter when he saw her scared. Then he laughed the way men do when they're enjoying being men, as though watching a soccer game with friends with a beer in his hand.

"Why don't you tell me about yourself?" His words were friendly but his tone was authoritarian.

Avellaneda wanted to run away, but the streets weren't much safer. On the contrary, outside there were those who preyed on the weaker and cooked them in metal containers. So she told him about her secretarial job in that company, and how she had been working overtime when everything began. When she went home, she found her house looted, her mother dead, and her father gone. She took only a few things, a blanket, clean clothes, the little food that was left, and returned to the warehouse. The houses and supermarkets were the most obvious targets, and the most dangerous places. She also brought a small radio that worked until the batteries ran out or the stations ceased broadcasting, which happened at more or less the same time. Since then she had lived there.

"There's nothing more to add," she said, forcing a smile. Her throat was dry and her thoughts strayed to the lemonade. Durruti ordered her to take him where she kept the animal feed. Avellaneda stood up and walked, feeling as though her joints were broken. She heard a blade slip out of its sheath. She felt it close behind her. Just as she opened the small door, the knife ripped into her right shoulder blade and tore through her rib cage. Blood and air gushed out of her at the same time. By the time her head hit the floor, she felt nothing. She couldn't see how he, rummaging inside the tank, found the bottle of pink lemonade. Obeying his instincts, he opened it and gulped it down.

The Return of Night

RENÉ ROQUET

Translated by ARMANDO GARCÍA

డ్స

T HE WORLD WAS conceived far away from the sun and the stars, inside a black cloak, where it received energy from a warm and generous ancestral womb. It had neither movement nor universe; it had no time because time was useless. It was an unblemished sphere, still in a single night without a morning to count the days. That is how darkness founded its kingdom, and it kept at bay a shadow that was never upset by the light. Everything belonged to it.

From the moment the planet took its final form, creatures and plants were placed on a vain surface. They were willing to be awoken, at any moment, by life. A starting breath, with their roots buried deep in the earth's flesh, they waited for the appearance of a sign, of a wind that would unveil their reason for being; to show them a reality different from the unyielding and impossible cocoon they occupied; to give them a beginning out of the automatic rhythm of their motionless volume. Mammals, insects and fish dozed in eternity, in the meaninglessness of things. They were newborn undistinguishable from their mothers breast. They half-dreamt of an accomplished dimension, while their eyes kept virgin a series of outside images. They inhabited a paradise. A planet different from the others that orbited the cosmic systems conducted by God. And in that throbbing space was a tree. A particular tree, enormous, at the foot of a hill. On it hung dozens of bats, waiting expectantly with their senses on edge, but with nothing to perceive. Without a pretext to move.

Until a stone fell.

At the top of the hill, the flapping of a fly, the contact of a body with another, or the exhalation of a feline's breath, created a wave that crashed on a rock near the shore, from which the stone broke off and rolled downhill, jumping and taking flight until it crossed in front of the tree where the bats hung. They felt it and opened their eyes. Time began for them and the kingdom of nothingness was no longer of the night, but belonged to these black animals with long fangs, who spread their wings for the first time and took flight, penetrating the clear sky.

They headed east. Together they traveled hundreds of fields and dark valleys, until the first bat to sense the stone stopped. There should an alternative, abandon freewheeling and discover if there is something else besides air, he said. They descended and noticed that their eyes did not need light. Nocturnal vision presented a unique spectacle: thousands of bodies lying like abundant fruits. The mammals flew around and touched them with their membranous wings and, little by little, poised on backs and hides. There were no rejections or tremors to the invader's weight. Nor for their lips' contact on skin. For the animated creatures it was easy to take a bite, bury their fangs into the flesh and experiment the unknown. They discovered novelty. The following bite endorsed a sense of pleasure, the surprise of warm blood running down the fat neck of one of the cows. The bats gathered to eat, to devour the victim. When it was emptied, they looked at themselves and their surroundings. Nothing had changed. The world continued paralyzed. The bats had just finished a life before it began, and nature did not complain, the eternal night did not weep, the other animals did not stop to condemn the murder.

The bats took once again to the heavens; they had just discovered that the surface sheltered a fruitful terrain belonging to them. From that moment, the bats' flight became slow and wide. They moved in a straight line to the east and fanned out towards the south and the north, looking for different landscapes, multitudes of beasts and fruits to bite. It was a steady advance of territorial conquest, lacking an enemy to subdue. It was enough to swoop down to the surface and proclaim their sovereignty over untouched property, where they, the small hirsute vertebrates with sharp ears, represented the omnipotence of a species beautiful and free from the hoards trapped in darkness. Any bat could take the lushest tree to sleep in, parade among giant beasts or crush an insect with the scorn of someone who already has everything. And then, calmly, continue to the east in search of more, of another space to reignite its curiosity and satisfy the sentence life had imposed on them:

to lick blood, to feel the saliva in its snout, to savor the juices of motionless organisms. This ritual was consummated by the taking over of others and accepting the earth's unselfish generosity. It consisted of the exploitation of an environment that did not resist abuse, even less that of a mass of thirsty creatures, of newborn, eager for sensations different than those they had in their past dreams of emptiness.

The bats' drive for appropriation was limitless and then, the sea appeared. The wall of water extended and became lost on the horizon, forcing them to halt their advance. The creatures were hit by the sound of the waves and shown the existence of other uncontainable powers, stronger than muscles and invisible radars. They found something that exceeded and overtook them, an enemy whose vitality they couldn't bite nor drain. A few went to inspect and discovered it was one more element that would not attack them nor contest their throne. However, with its disclosure, they were forced to react in a different manner. The bats began to revise their experiences to see if among them was a strategy that would help them get around the problem. Since they found nothing that would help them continue in their conquest, they thought of two possible solutions: They would turn around, or realize, at that very moment, whom they were. They had learned to quench their hunger and curiosity and they had succeeded in taking over the earth, the skies and the beings yet unborn. Being themselves was now important, but they needed to control their plundering instinct.

Sitting on the sand, the night creatures carefully looked at themselves. Although they knew themselves to be different, they accepted their collectivity. They were bats. The ones chosen to rule. And if they had to learn anything about themselves, they would have to get closer to what most resembled their being, and this was in the gender that had accompanied them since leaving the tree that gave them life.

Without doubting, a female bat stretched her wings to stroke a male's face and with her long fingers absorbed the essence of her species. There followed a pleasure that she did not wish to consume, but possess and nurture within her to transform her into something unique, an internal lighthouse capable of lighting up the soul. They carefully joined their limbs, sweat stimulated their sense of smell. They let the hairiness of their skin enter the intimate space of the other in a dark caressing of their bodies, an initiation that led to an instinctive penetration, full of doubts and curious to know what more there was beyond the opened female and the erect male penis, which entered nervously and with haste. The bats filled the beach with their forms. They swayed, they screeched. They imitated the rhythm of the tide that died on the sand and returned to the ocean's lungs to be reborn in a new breath that extended again towards the coasts and the sharp rocks, where it exploded in the shape of foam and millions of white drops.

The male sheltered his mate with an embrace, while he confessed in her ear the sensations he had noticed since opening his eyes. She believed him, she threw away the fragments that reminded her of her own history and wove an essence renovated with the leftovers of his discourse, with the same pleasure, with the same echoes that the sex between her legs had left. The intercourse was an exchange of profound impressions, like their exploration of that boundary. The bats became a community, a loving shape; they had an awakening of themselves. From their shared emotions an impulse was born, a decision that did not come from their natural tendency towards flight but from an ode to each other's partner. In pairs they rose and took to the sky; they turned several times and then moved far across the ocean, increasing their speed. The creatures felt a defiant vigor. They wanted to reach the other side of infinity without touching the liquid surface.

They glided through the dense skies. They had the face of freedom drawn on their extremities, which they flapped gracefully. Below, the waves repeated themselves while the salty smell rose, striking their noses. The horizon was visible in the distance, bathed in dark blue. Everything seemed possible and within reach: until one of them, tired from having covered hundreds of kilometers, fell. The lack of food and constant exercise abated him. The animal sank into the water, and with him he took the courage to reach the unknown. They had to halt the journey and ask themselves if the enterprise was not overwhelming. Some thought of returning. But with such distance and without land in sight, it was difficult to know where the nearest shore was. Nor could they be sure that there would be something on the other side, a virgin paradise with solid ground. The arguments and screams started. Part of the group turned around, after having scratched and bitten those whom they had earlier made love to at the beach. The majority of them continued the journey, propping each other up, pushing each other on, relieving the pain with hopeful screams. They knew that they could not trust the sea, that their wings were their only guarantee for survival. Nonetheless, they recognized they had reached a limit and as they progressed, they had to move away from each other, make room and abandon their support for one another. The debacle became clear as they started to lunge at and devour the bats plummeting to the ocean. They could do nothing else. The atmosphere had become so strained that the feeling union and belonging had fragmented into personal battles, setting the scene for their burial or their redemption.

The flock was reduced to half and then to a quarter. The flight had turned into a pilgrimage towards insanity. The species born to rule over the world discovered its true dimension and a power limited by a reality that had lost its meaning, blurred by incomprehensible energies not governed by mortality. The bats surrendered themselves to the unknown and their ignorance, to continue their journey. They did not know if the ocean was above and the sky below or if they were really advancing. The movement of their wings was the only constant in the distorted night.

At one point, in their last glimmer of consciousness, they thought they were dead, a contradictory notion, that kept them alive. They had seized the idea to such an extent that when they reached the shore, they did not recognize the end of their heroic deed. They had to crash against the sand, the palm trees and the cliffs to return to their normal state of mind. Their recovered vision revealed a natural richness even more marvelous than the one they had already known. With the little energy they had left, they dedicated themselves to satisfying those desires they weren't able to quench during their odyssey, including sleep and motionlessness. Their impetus made them forget quickly what they had lived over the waves and to feel once again the necessity to dominate paradise, to gain territory for their glorious species. This instinct was championed by a surprising event that drove a different course on the static planet: the females generated life. They gave birth among the eternal shadows. All around the females were crying younglings, they consoled them by breastfeeding and offering them the flesh of the inexhaustible surface. The new found continent was conquered from east to west, by the frenzy of the chosen and their fledglings, they squashed grapes to observe the trickling of the juice, hung on branches to see if they could stand their weight. Their advance was slow, constant and without obstruction.

Until they returned to the sea, once again.

This time, the bats did not lie down on the sand to make love, nor did they think about the limit of their power. They decided to return. Five of them stayed behind staring at the horizon, listening to the breaking of the waves. There had to be something on the other side of the waters. An answer that gave meaning to their impulsive movement, to their necessity to possess whatever stood in front of them. The five of them took flight and went deep into the ocean, into the proven lunacy of the eternal journey. On this crossing, only one was able to reach the other shore. He touched solid ground and as tribute, he pulled a fruit from a shrub; he ate one half and made an offering to the sea with the other. He then retook his flight to the east. On his voyage he discovered that the lands were not virginal, that they were populated by his fellow brethren. The bats that had abandoned them on the first crossing had succeeded in returning to the earliest continent and recovering it. He also discovered that they had the same gift of giving life, and that their offspring followed by their side, persuing the desires of their parents.

The bat continued on his way trying to find something else other than instinctive depredation. He knew he was getting closer, that soon he would find a reason that would explain why he could not stop his peregrination. Then he recognized a figure. Before him stood the tree that engendered life. He had reached the beginning of everything. He descended and caressed its trunk, looking for a sign, anything that would give meaning to his existence. At that moment he felt dizzy, then a powerful shiver, stronger than flight, than the ability to reproduce, than the ocean's currents. The world trembled. Half-walking, half flying he climbed the hill from which the stone had broken off. At the top, he saw the valley of his beginning, extending in a single plane towards the east. On the horizon, he was able to see what was happening, something terrible: a red line, followed by a glowing blue, gave way to an enormous yellow sphere rolling towards him, setting fire with its flame of life the sleeping species it touched as it smashed its way through. The animals of creation finally inhaled air and exhaled in screams, screams that traveled the earth.

The bat could watch no longer. His eyes burned in the intense light. He was becoming blind. He had to turn around and flee. But the heavenly star king insisted on following him, in devouring his domain of darkness. In his escape he found others of his kind that did not know what to do and who, in the confusion, left everything behind including their children and their partners. He saw them through shadows, witnessed the collapse of his kingdom. Desperate, he flew to the ground and took two abandoned little ones. With them he made his way towards a cave he discovered at the western end of the cliff. He went inside looking for the escaping blackness. As a final act, he covered the younglings with his wings and waited. When he felt safe, he uncovered them. They did not understand and stared at him imploring an explanation. The bat did not know what to tell them.

Three Messages and a Warning in the Same Email

ANÁ CLAVEL

Translated by ELSY JACKSON

ॐ

Inhabiting the house of another
Is indeed a strange experience.

—JOSÉ LUIS CUEVAS

DEAR SAMUEL:

When I moved into your house, I didn't care about throwing my plans into the wastebasket. I had thought about going on vacation to the beach or taking that photography class that I had told you about, but this year's vacation was added to those of previous years that never happened. The truth is that although you had not pressured me at all, I would have offered to stay in your house. After all, I thought, we were friends. I am writing you now in memory of what remains of that friendship. Your scholarship for advanced studies in England (do you remember how much I too struggled to obtain it?) is about to come to an end, and, therefore, your return must be imminent. But don't come back, Samuel. Stay there. Didn't you tell me the last time you called on the telephone about all the opportunities they had offered you to stay in Liverpool? The reason you give for rejecting them seems to me to have no rational basis. Don't you realize that you're in love with Lorena? I, Luis, ask this of you; you remember Luis, right? He's the one who sat in your place for your exams in analytical geometry and chemical analysis. Samuel, don't come back. We had good times back then, didn't we? I used to go to your house to give you the notes you were missing from the classes you had missed. Poor Doña Carmen was horrified when she found out about your absences, but you always calmed her with a kiss. Do you remember? At that time I only had access to your bedroom, and every once and a while, the dining room, where, of course, the only mirror in the whole house is situated. Now it's different and though I can open all the doors in the house, I don't do it. I only use those that lead to the kitchen and to your room. I think that when your mother was alive you used to do the same: in the mornings during breakfast and at daybreak when you would come back from your parties.

Perhaps you'll be surprised when I tell you that my lifestyle is about the same as when you lived here. Luis has changed so dramatically that now it's most likely that you will no longer recognize him. Or perhaps you will recognize too much in him. I expect that this one proof will be sufficient for you to understand what I mean. Remember the Jimmy Hendrix record I bought for you when you turned twenty-one? Yes, that collector's edition with the cover with all the naked girls on it that you couldn't find anywhere. Despite your repeatedly insisting that he was the best strummer in the world, he never pleased me much, and every time you invited me to listen to him I preferred to invent just about any excuse and go home. Now, however, I really like him. But don't think I suddenly realized my lack of good taste; rather it's that I feel I have an in-depth knowledge of the record. What's more, the first time I played it alone I could specify without any difficulty which tone followed another, the order and combinations of musical instruments, and each part of the harmonies without any difficulty.

It seems to me, nonetheless, that I am not complying with the purpose of this message, because although I have talked to you about some of the things that are happening here, there are others that I am not completely sure of and I prefer to confirm my suspicions before sharing them with you. I hope you don't mind . . .

2

SAMUEL:

At the rate I am going I am quite afraid that I will not finish this second letter, either. Do you want reasons? I don't want to know them completely. Do you want apologies? I'm sorry, I'm sorry, I'm sorry, I'm sorry, I'm sorry (as many as are required to constitute one thousand, fill them in yourself). Seriously, if your girlfriends from the club get here on time, as we agreed for today's party, it's most likely that I will not finish it: and, obviously, I won't send it to you in that case.

You know what? In the beginning I couldn't understand how you got along without mirrors, because other than the one that covers the dining room from one end to the other, there is no other mirror in the whole house, and you coming downstairs at midday half-asleep, running the risk of slipping, didn't seem reasonable to me. My stubby beard, the "prickly pear cactus," as you used to call it, is bushy now, and it has become clear to me why you always wore a heavy beard. Still, the lack of mirrors continues to puzzle me (I think I may have even mentioned it to you in my previous letter), and I have formulated various hypotheses, none convincing me completely.

Chewed up as if by a rat by idiotic conjectures that led me nowhere, I resolved to catch the subject by the tail, stick it in an empty jar, and throw it in the trash.

The answer came later of its own accord. It was sufficient to carry on a busy night life (followed by dreadful mornings) to understand it. No one likes to look at himself at such an early hour in such a depressing state. It's for this reason that I also avoid the only mirrors in the house now, at least right after waking. My entire manner of dressing has changed as a result, and I take greater care to be presentable. What's good about it is that the girls from the company have taken notice and they even flirt with me. I'm not joking. It was about time they should recognize me as someone other than just Samuel's friend.

I keep the house in the same condition as you had it before you went away. The maid keeps coming once a week, as when you were here. As you can see, your departure hasn't changed the routine around here.

But there is something I should ask your forgiveness for. Remember my weak and puny body? Well, I have put on a few pounds, so your clothes fit me perfectly, including your sporting attire. So I have taken the tennis rackets and made use of your membership in the country club. After all, don't you agree that it's best that someone takes advantage of it? Don't jump to conclusions. It was not an easy choice for me. The first time that I dared to go to the club I was nervous, afraid that at any moment they would discover me. Nothing happened, however.

I imagine that despite the cold and the nuisance of the advanced courses you are taking, you must be having a great time. Has your enviable tan faded yet? They say that there are heated pools there and an artificial beach that is illuminated at night. Do you go to those places? I've got a nice tan now. It's just about as good as yours, thanks to your club membership and your condo in Cuernavaca.

Are you enjoying yourself over there? Why even question it! Knowing you, it's a sure bet. And that's another reason why you absolutely must stay. Take advantage of the opportunities you mentioned and please don't come back.

3

YOU WOULD HAVE gotten my earlier messages last week, but since I never sent them, I can't blame the Internet. I will include them both with this one, which I am hurriedly writing. I am sending all three of them to you because repeating the two previous ones with all the facts that I know now and did not know then is embarrassing for those who hate the epistolary genre, as you can imagine. If it were not that I know your shouting voice in the same way that I am beginning to be accustomed to mine, I would call you on the phone to put an end to all this. Anyway, since time is short and our needs are equally urgent, I will only briefly mention what happened. Do you remember the last time we talked on the phone? You told me then that what kept you from staying in Liverpool was your desire to see Lorena again, that your breaking up with her had been a mistake. I understand what you mean now. Before I only knew her through your descriptions, but when I was writing the message before this one, she came over with the other girls I had been expecting. She was prepared to make up with you. She said she had been at the beach for a while at your recommendation, to settle her nerves, before coming to visit the house. Just as with the records and so many other things, it was enough for me to see her to recognize her and understand what had transpired between you, that is, between us. You're a damned liar. She wasn't to blame. You wanted to protect your pride, no doubt, but when Luis wrote you not to come back he knew what he was talking about. You'd better pay attention to him. Your return would have disastrous consequences. Now then, that's all I have to say. I don't want to arrive late to my wedding. Pay attention to me and stay abroad. Don't think of the properties of yours that I've seized, think of Lorena, for if you truly love her you must comprehend the irreparable shock it would cause her to learn that there are two Samuels.

The President without Organs

PEPE ROJO

Translated by CHRIS N. BROWN

൧ჩ

Wednesday, March 13.

"I'M VERY FLATTERED," said the president when he got the news that the best surgical team was charged with removing the abscess of fat that had formed in his rectum and provoked his strange behavior in recent months. "It's difficult to sit with a ping-pong ball stuck in my butt," he said, smiling as always, the president. The Opposition sent him written apologies.

Fernando Guerra went down in the elevator of the smart building, concentrating on the voice that came out of the intercom and told clean jokes to entertain the passengers. When the elevator doors opened, Fernando Guerra encountered his workmates.

"I knew it," said Lucas Rivero, director of public relations, "I've been having trouble sitting lately, but this afternoon I have an appointment with the proctologist."

The four people surrounding him nodded, preoccupied. One of them gave Rivero the doctor's telephone number. Fernando Guerra looked at them, pensive. *That's why I've been feeling sick,* he thought while squeezing his intenstines, trying to detect any abnormality, *maybe I need to get myself a checkup.*

Thursday, April 14.

THE PRESIDENT NO LONGER HAS FUR ON HIS TONGUE

The presidency communicated yesterday that the tumor that had invaded the mouth of the president was successfully removed. "Because it was a high-risk operation," continued the newscaster, "we decided not to televise it."

The tumor, known scientifically as a *bezoar worm*, is normally found in the stomach. Its characteristics include the uncontrollable growth of hair and nails in the cancerous mass, and a strong odor due to the particles of food trapped in it.

The doctors were unable to explain the growth's appearance inside the mouth cavity. We asked this newspaper's psychic, the great Mento.

"The president is a special person, having spent many years perfecting the technique of speaking without the ideas passing through the brain," he told us before entering into a ninety-minute trance. "Perhaps because of this, now the president does not need food to pass through his stomach."

Heriberto Néstor continued with his lecture:

"Politics is the vanguard of fiction," he said while pretending to read some notes that were in reality an endless game of tic tac toe. "The greatest narrative innovations, the best stylistic developments and the almost instantaneous access to the mass media have made it the most noble of all genres."

"Besides entertaining and moving us," he continued, while trying to peek between the skirt pleats of a student sitting in front of him, "politics as a literary genre has managed to change the economy of passion. The most precious product of our society generates utility thanks to the surplus value of suffering, and allows us to redeem our sins by means of the suffering of our democratic representatives."

The question and answer session was especially boring. Heriberto Néstor was telling himself he was losing his charm when he left the lecture hall surrounded by fiftysomething maestras. He just wanted to go home and read one of the comics he'd bought. Before, he'd never had a lecture from which he hadn't left in the arm of a young chick from the university. He needed to look for more controversial themes: if Néstor had learned anything it was that there was nothing like counterculture and scandal to get regular sex.

Friday, May 15.

"MY DAUGHTER HAS magical powers," the president said with great seriousness, "and it's a public fact since I assumed control of the nation. The immoral accusations made against me are the product of ignorance." At that moment, a tear scurried across the made-up cheek of our head of state.

"The sensibilities are distinct," he continued, "and extraordinary persons cannot hope that their conduct will be understood by the masses. The relationship I have with my daughter is intimate and strong. In consulting her, I always have the welfare of the nation in mind, and these sessions have solved economic problems before."

The photos of the president and his daughter totally absorbed in what appeared to be sexual play were sold to all the media in accordance with the freedom of information law.

BREAKING NEWS: The president had a nervous breakdown five minutes ago. The causes are unknown. Don't change the channel and we'll keep you informed.

Claudia Pelufo entered the ladies' room. Something she ate hadn't sat with her well, but any sort of commentary on the food in a five-star restaurant could provoke a lawsuit against the customer. She entered the bathroom and heard a male voice coming out of one of the stalls. Claudia Pelufo had never gotten used to the presence of transsexuals in ladies' rooms. She heard a second voice, female. Claudia Pelufo tried to listen to the conversation.

"It's the original, it's unique," said the male voice. "You know you can confide in me."

"Can I touch it?" answered the woman.

"First you have to pay."

Curiosity killed the cat, thought Claudia.

"I don't have a better amulet than this one," continued the transsexual. "It's not every day you can buy a bezoar worm of a living president. They didn't say it on the air, but the tumor developed an eye. In addition to the tumor, I am going to sell you the third eye of a national hero."

They started laughing, and something fell on the floor. Claudia Pelufo crouched down to see under the door. She leaned in to see two pairs of legs and an object in a bag. The tumor was a ball of hair. In the center of this mass, an eye was fixed on Claudia Pelufo. She felt a charge of pleasure run down her spinal column and lodge between her legs. She held back a moan and exited quickly. Blushing, she sat at the table with her husband.

The bathroom door opened and a smiling woman came out, walking quickly.

"Look," Claudia Pelufo said to her husband. "Here we have a happy woman."

Saturday, June 16.

IN THE FOURTH week of national grief over the constant danger of death lurking over our president, his situation does not appear to have improved. How can we forget the touching images that the surgical camera grabbed while traveling through the moist and pulsing intestines of our dear president? It's no surprise that in a recent survey he was considered the greatest chief of state Mexico has ever had, beating Luis Donaldo Colosio in the polls for the first time. They have installed TV monitors in all the government offices so as not to deprive the employees of their right to complete information. The political body of our nation convulses with the rhythm of the peristaltic movements and ventricle drumming of our beloved president.

Martha Garcés was happy. She'd never felt that way around all
the people she lived among. You could see it in in the metro,
looking in the eyes of all the other passengers without fear of
being misinterpreted. All had the same thing on their mind: the
well-being of the president. The Secretary of Cults and Religions
had made a desperate call to the nation: every three days, conduct
mass rites of the most popular religions and belief systems of the
entire world, hoping that one would have a positive effect and
cure the ill health of the president.

Of particular interest to Martha Garcés had been the doc-
trine of the Enneagram. She had enjoyed the shamanistic operation that had been performed on the president. A few bells rang
over the loudspeaker of the metro car. Martha Garcés waited a
few moments to see the reactions of the other passengers. They
all kneeled, facing the same direction. Martha copied them.
It was rather difficult to determine the correct direction of
Mecca.

Sunday, July 17.

NATIONAL TIME-OUT DAY.

Monday, August 18.

"GOOD MORNING, MEXICO! We start the week with excellent
news. Last night, the president recovered his consciousness. His
closest aides commented that in addition to feeling strong, he

was in good spirits. Before going in front of the cameras, the president, always careful about his appearance, asked to be left alone with his makeup artist. When he came before the cameras, the president intoned our traditional anthem: 'The King.' We'll be back with exclusive images after this commercial break."

Carla D'Alessio communicated for years with the spirit of the deceased Gina Montes and could not hide her desperation in front of the altar in which the monitor incessantly repeated the classic opening of the program Gina made famous. Although everyone had seen the president's song, the experts said there had been no improvement. Gina Montes couldn't communicate with her for some time. Life did not smile on Carla D'Alessio.

She waited a few seconds so that Gina's words flooded her head and took possession of her. She took the knapsack stuffed with cotton balls holding beads of sweat of the president. Her friend, a nurse in the Santa Fe Hospital, had gotten them. Carla sold them with pendants of the Virgin of Guadalupe outside the Basilica. She turned to see the beautiful body of Gina while moving rhythmically in the monitor, conjured through time thanks to the electricity. She sighed and walked to the door. She still had to pay for the operation by means of which her name changed from Carlos to Carla.

Tuesday, August 19.

"I WANT A son before I die," said the president, agonized, to the doctors surrounding him. The president had been unable to get an erection for three years, which made it somewhat complicated to obtain a semen sample the natural way. The president had four daughters and not a single son. It was hoped that advances in genetics would enable the conception of a baby boy by the First Lady, who was ready to spend the coming months in bed rest, as the pregnancy would be high-risk.

"If this is the final sacrifice I can make," she said with tears in her eyes, "I will do it happily, for him and for our country."

The Congress for the Reconstruction of the Nation assembled by the Opposition had been a hit with the media. Pedro Negrete felt something was missing. The opposition parties prepared an emergency plan in case the president passed away. The nihilists asserted that the president was not sick, that it was all a lie. The pessimist faction said the sale of the president's organs was financing the fiscal deficit. There wasn't a single fact that could be proven.

The executive-privilege dining trucks discharged a succulent dinner. The president, moved by the concern of his rivals, had paid for a performance of Circus Atayde to liven up the closing of the Congress.

Valentin Allende came closer and said: "We are going to be delayed in political questions; in Europe and North America you still can't talk of making public the lives of the presidents as an electoral strategy, the future was in religions, for which . . ." Valentin interrupted his discourse, looked in the eyes of Pedro Negrete and asked: "You're still worried about Sandra, right?"

Pedro Negrete nodded his head. Sandra Pelayo had been his right hand during the last three years, and his lover for the last two. Sandra had said to him that she was sick of arguing and achieving nothing. This night she had returned to the capital, where she put herself on the list of candidates that were going to try to obtain the presidential ejaculate.

Wednesday, September 20.

THE NATION IS in mourning. The president has died. Long live the president. In the next hour we will have interviews, commentaries and a profile of the life of our deceased president. The team of geneticists assures us that they will make the greatest effort to make the president the first dead man to conceive a child.

The specialists are preparing to conduct the autopsy. They seek mystic-religious, psychological, extraterrestrial and physiological causes of death. All the specialists have signed exclusive contracts with this station for the live broadcast of the operations. You'll only have the compete information if you stay tuned. The president has died. Long live the president.

The Transformist

HORACIO SENTÍES MADRID

Translated by EDUARDO JIMÉNEZ MAYO
and JOSÉ ALEJANDRO FLORES

For Bruno Estañol, with admiration

ॐ

October 15, 1923

ONE ALWAYS CHOOSES how one dies, and, in the end, death is nothing but a transformation: this idea is an obsession of Monsieur Poulenc, who swears he knows the day and time of his death. Perhaps in the future someone will decide to die a gaucho's death, dagger in hand, somewhere in the remote south of Argentina. All my miseries began when Sarah died, this past March, but not until now have I dared to write about my sorrows. Her funeral was attended by one hundred fifty thousand people.

I took some flowers to her grave in Père Lachaise. After leaving them, I felt a terrible pain on the right side of my head as I bumped into one of the stone arches while roaming about the grounds.

I was eleven when I first saw her. My father had taken me to the Odéon Theater: which years later she utilized as a convalescent hospital, caring for the war wounded, an effort earning her the Legion of Honor. Her performance as Queen Elizabeth, interpreting Moreau's film script, was superb. A couple of years later I witnessed her transform into Jeanne Doré. The beauteous Oceanids, legendary daughters of the Titans Oceanus and Tethys, must have paled in comparison to her splendor. In 1887 when she appeared at the Grand National Theater of Mexico as "a beautiful stranger," her performance in *La Dame aux Camelias* earned her glowing praise from the critics: "We were fortunate to be visited by one of Virgil's goddesses, shrouded by a dense veil of mystery. More than a woman, she is a burning bush." After her right leg was amputated, following years of suffering, I could no longer see her on stage. Unlike other actresses her mannerisms were natural. I hated the gross overacting of her contemporaries. She delved into the mood of her characters: every intonation, every gesture, was uniquely suited to her role. Most intriguing was her stage interpretation of "dying"—stammers, groans, and agony during which the cobalt blue of her eyes and her blond hair seemed to glow and then fade. Perhaps she slept in a coffin so as to be closer to death in life. The photographs of Monsieur Nadar and his son capture her practicing this custom.

For over three years her spirit pursued me closely in all my whereabouts; every woman's face became hers. The countenances of the women around me invariably reflected her features, and she took possession of their thoughts and feelings as well.

Terribly, unavoidably, I succumbed to her spell. I was forced to evade my places of work—the coffee shop, the factory, the restaurant, private homes—hoping to escape from her invasive presence. But to no avail. I took to sleeping in the shelters of the Salvation Army to elude her roving spirit. When I looked at my mother, in a matter of seconds her face began to assume the appearance of the woman with "the golden voice." Not only my mother, mind you, but all the people with whom I associated suffered this transformation; even their clothes mimicked Sarah's: camisoles, bustles, corsets, crinolines, petticoats. A few days ago a begging girl knocked at the door. Upon seeing her face assume Sarah's features, I decided to lock her in the shelter pantry, thinking maybe that way I could get rid of her forever. I even contemplated killing the child. I went out, but the first face I saw became that of my persecutor. I decided to return to free the little girl, who was crying incessantly when I arrived. The abducted child was sitting on the floor, hugging her knees, when I opened the door. Her face morphed into Sarah's, momentarily expressing the actress' mocking laughter, before she rose to her feet and ran from the place.

November 6, 1924

LATELY THE SITUATION has become intolerable. Sarah's mother and aunt were women of ill repute. She inherited her real name from her Aunt Rosine. Neither she nor her sisters knew who her parents were. Her sister Jeanne dedicated herself to the courtesan's life. But she was committed to the Pitié-Salpêtrière hospital under the care of Professor Charcot for the treatment of neurosis and morphine addiction. Why is it that women of ill repute, patterned after Manon from the homonymous *opéra comique*, always seem to end up confined in Pitié-Salpêtrière? As a child, Sarah remained in a boarding school in Auteuil near the homes of Bergson and Proust, and later in the Grandchamp convent school near Versailles.

She wanted to devote her life to God, but her mother influenced her to be a high-class courtesan. At first, she refused. But after her abandonment by Prince de Ligne while pregnant with Maurice, her libertinism began. Monsieur Hugo chose her for the role of the Queen in the revival of *Ruy Blas,* and ever since then her name was associated with his, as it would be with Monsieur Doré and Monsieur D'Annunzio. Monsieur Nadar photographed her naked on several occasions. Her marriage to Monsieur Damal was a sham. Both were exemplars of infidelity. Only another morphine addict would have thought to marry her. Marie Colombier recently provoked a scandal by publishing Sarah's *Les voyages en Amérique* and *Mémoires*, for which a three-month prison sentence was imposed in response to public outrage at the materials' supposed indecency. The gallant life of the actress is revealed in them in all its grandeur.

Sarah's sister has also begun to haunt me atrociously. I am the only woman in my family who lives in chastity. I have been able to keep away foolish men with the assistance of a skin condition that makes me look prematurely aged yet affords me the opportunity to remain purer than my sisters. Perhaps this is why Sarah's sister has chosen to invade my thoughts and compel me nocturnally to make dirty and immoral contact with myself of which I am ashamed.

December 3, 1926

HOW HAS SARAH accomplished her postmortem persecution of me? I can only explain it through Spiritualism. Allan Kardec in *The Spirits' Book* explains how the dead can come into contact with the living. I firmly believe that this is possible, and I am joined in this belief by the likes of Ravaisson-Mollien, Monsieur Lachelier, a Scottish writer named Conan Doyle, and even the recently assassinated Mexican president. I have attended the performances of magicians Erik Weisz and Erik Jan Hanussen and I have read about mentalism in search of a solution to this martyrdom. Despite the spectacular cures of James Braid and Professor Charcot through hypnosis, in my case this treatment has had no effect whatsoever. After meeting Monsieur Hoffman, the magnetizer, I turned to the glass harmonica for assistance. I experienced a temporary improvement similar to that of Maria Theresia von Paradis, the woman who despite her blindness managed to play concerts by Mozart and who was treated by Monsieur Mesmer himself. I decided to abandon my treatment regime after a few days because Sarah appeared again, ubiquitously, and because many have witnessed that those who hear the sound of the glass harmonica, an invention of Benjamin Franklin, eventually grow as insane as Lucia di Lammermoor.

December 9, 1926

DEAREST PAUL:

A new patient came to me a few days ago. She is twenty-seven, employed as a domestic servant, and her appearance is a little coarse. She has striven to develop a modicum of culture and is a fervent believer in mentalism. She possesses the firm belief that the former actress "The Great Sarah Bernhardt" and her sister are pursuing her by imposing their facial and physical characteristics on the people with whom she associates. During the course of my interview with her, for example, she mentioned that I and the interns who accompanied me had assumed their visages. I have written to our colleagues Capgras and Reboul-Lachaux; but the woman who sought help from me suffers from an illness opposite to the one in which they specialize. I always appreciate your valuable opinions and hope you might shed some light on this experience.

> Best wishes and warmest affections,
> G. Fail

December 20, 1926

MY DEAREST FRIEND:

I have been thinking about the woman whom you refer to in your letter and I do not have a plausible explanation for it, but it awakened in me some reflections which I shall make an effort to present to you. It seems to me that the whole problem lies in the understanding one has of reality. Parmenides said that the universe, including time and space, and perhaps we ourselves, are nothing but an appearance or a succession of appearances. Thomas Carlyle, in *Sartor Resartus*, promotes a similar view, only that for the Scot the whole universe is a charade. Similarly, Bishop Berkeley holds that matter consists of a series of perceptions whose reality would be inconceivable without consciousness. John Locke would reduce reality to our perceptions and feelings, even more precisely, to our memories and perceptions of those memories; matter exists because the five senses make it so. All this establishes that the nature of the reality of objects is not contained in their primary characteristics, rather in the perceptions that we are able to create on the basis of their secondary characteristics.

Now I shall mention some new ideas that my father-in-law, Paul Sollier, related to me and which are relevant to this case. Remember that my father-in-law was a disciple of Professor Charcot and some twenty years ago wrote a book called *Les phénomène d'autoscopy*. He worked primarily on the phenomenon of memory. In fact, one of his patients whom he treated at Boulogne-Billancourt wrote a novel, *À la recherche du temps perdu*, inspired by the concepts in my father-in-law's scientific essay, *Les troubles de la mémoire*. In the novel of which I speak, the son of Professor Adrien Proust wrote that true reality exists only in the mind; consequently, the reality we perceive depends only secondarily on the objects and circumstances surrounding us but primarily on the perceptions and memories that we have of them. The unfortunate woman you describe, relentlessly pursued by the Bernhardt sisters, represents a pathological example of this psychological truth. What a dreadful life she must lead, tormented by the guises of deceased souls. I do not think you can convince her otherwise, for her perceptions fashioned from powerful memories are as real to her as yours are to you. Our friend Henri Bergson, akin to Proust, has devoted much of his attention to the analysis of reality. In fact his book *Matière et mémoire* takes up the subject directly. For Henri, the brain registers movements, sensations, and perceptions, but "pure memory" refers to a spiritual reservoir of images of the past continuously reshaped according to present conditions and necessities. Objects must be situated and conceptualized to ensure the stability of their representation. Man relies on such representations to make sense of reality and yet he laughs at them, knowing them to be a caricature or deformation of reality as such. The impressionist painters of the past century and now the surrealists remind us of the treachery of human consciousness. Their work speaks volumes on the condition of your patient besieged by omnipresent images of the Bernhardt sisters.

> *Receive my most cordial greetings,*
> *Paul Courbon*
> *Chef de Service*
> *Hôpital Sainte Anne Paris*
> *1 Rue Cabanis*

January 3, 1927

DEAREST PAUL:

Your reflections are interesting but perhaps a bit too positivist given this woman's mystical nature. I would like to discuss her case further with you and for you to meet her, perhaps this Friday afternoon. Afterward we might attend the Olympia Theatre, which, as you recall, stands opposite to the home and studio of Monsieur Nadar on the Boulevard des Capucines. A retrospective film will be shown there of Leopoldo Frégoli, the great quick-change artist who said that art is life and life is transformation.

> *Until then,*
> *G. Fail*

The Drop

CLAUDIA GUILLÉN

Translated by LEAH LEONE

For Fernando León Guillén

ॐ

T HE DROP that fell discreetly
and hesitantly, careful not to disturb Ana's rest, had become part
of the room's ambience. As she had been doing every morning
for years now, Clara went upstairs to her daughter's room with
a bottle of IV fluid. This time, though, she was accompanied by
a young man to whom she spoke incessantly.

"See her, Doc? It's just like I said. My daughter's been like
this for five whole years. She doesn't move. She just sits there
and stares. But that's not all: every night, sitting just like that,
she closes her eyes and doesn't open them again till the next
morning."

The doctor interrupted her, irritated by Clara's passive acceptance of her daughter's illness.

"I'm sorry, ma'am, but I cannot understand why you promote your daughter's vegetative state."

"What state?" she asked.

"Vegetative, ma'am." A brief silence gave him just enough time to observe this small woman who seemed weak and wore an ironic expression, and he felt somewhat sorry for her. "Look, what I mean to say is you should do something so that Ana stops sitting there in that chair, not moving, not speaking, as if she were a vegetable."

Away from her body flew Clara's two small hands, moving as fast as her mouth.

"Ah, Doc, don't say that, please. You have no idea what we went through to finally figure out the trick with the drop. Don't look at me like that; you may not believe it, but that drop keeps my Ana alive. Yes, really, that water gives her life."

Meanwhile, the doctor listened resignedly to the old woman's story, helping her place the IV on its stand, unaware of how his assistance was making his residency there take on a new reality.

"Listen, one day Ana received a letter that told her her boyfriend was dead. She cried and cried. Her eyes were drained. She wouldn't eat or come out of her room. She had me and her father, God rest his soul, really worried . . . but we decided not to bother her. Until one day, we didn't hear her crying or making any noise at all. You can imagine my distress. I ran up the stairs to see what was wrong, and when I came into the room, I found her sitting in the corner, watching some water drop from the ceiling. I asked her what she was doing there, but she didn't answer my questions, even when I shouted at her.

"Then we called a doctor, who said she was in a state of shock

because of the loss she'd suffered. Ah, Doc, right away we had
the leak fixed, just like the doctor told us to. He said that would
make her come out of it, but wouldn't you know, instead of
coming out of it, she started dying on us. She aged a lot, and
was getting worse every day. Then I remembered how peaceful
she looked with the drop. So I ran to her dad's room to find one
of those droppers he used for his medicine and I stood in front
of my daughter and I started dripping drops into the bottle.

"Miraculously, almost right away she started getting better,
and the age started leaving her skin. For months or maybe years,
I don't even know anymore, Doctor, my husband and me took
turns with the dropper until one fine day, on my way home
from the grocery store, it occurred to me to stop in that store
on the corner where all the doctors are.

"First I explained what was wrong with my Ana and they
looked at me like I was crazy, and probably just to get me off
their backs they said that what I wanted was a drop, and that
bottles could hold a lot of them. I knew they were making fun of
me, but I didn't care, especially when one of those guys showed
me the little hose that comes out of the bottle that makes the
water come out drop by drop.

"I bought ten of those bottles, that now I know are for IV
fluid, and I was sure that everything had changed, and it did,
Doctor, everything changed. I know it's hard to believe, but
from that moment on we could rest: her father, when he was
alive, me, and, of course, my Ana. If you insist on studying her,
go ahead. I've already lost count of how many doctors have come,
and left as fast as they got here. And don't think I'm saying that
because I have some kind of chip on my shoulder. It's not that.
I'm just sure that you're gonna get tired of this too, just like all
the other doctors—although, you know, I have a good feeling

about you. On top of it all, I'll make you a deal: if in six months you haven't managed to make my Ana come back, then you'll knock it off. Because we both know my daughter's not going to get better."

Without looking at him, she turned toward Ana and, winking, said, "Right, honey?"

She left the room while the doctor looked around himself: the old wood floor, the bed, and a huge mirror shaped like a full moon, reflecting Ana's entire body. She was dressed in white, with her curly hair falling over her shoulders, and her discreet beauty, that filled the room, respectful of the sound and movement of the drop.

As time passed, the doctor became more and more familiar with the house. First he set about studying any reaction Ana could have to anything other than the drop. There was nothing. Regardless, he decided that music and literature would be the beginning of a common language with Ana. As for Clara, she believed herself witness to the devotion the doctor showed to her daughter.

One morning, the malicious mother went upstairs to change the IV bottle. Upon entering Ana's room she found the doctor reading aloud. Without a second thought, she interrupted him midsentence and said, "See, Doc? I told you you weren't gonna fix anything; and today the six months that we agreed upon are up."

Annoyed, the doctor looked up from his book. Seeing him, the old lady realized how far removed she was from the atmosphere that now reigned in the room, and she left like a child caught misbehaving.

She had not yet shut the door when the doctor said to Ana,

"See? Your mother is making fun of me. She doesn't think you hear me, but I know you do."

Imperturbable, Ana stayed in the same position.

The doctor raised his voice. "Don't you understand that today is my last day with you and that if you don't stop with the drop and the silence I won't be able to keep coming to see you?"

At that moment, Ana's head turned as if she were a doll on a string, and with a hoarse voice said, "Doctor, water evaporates, leaving behind only silence. It neither ages nor dies."

She immediately returned to the same position in which she had been. The young doctor looked at her disconsolately at first, but a few minutes later a slight smile drew itself across his face. He said nothing else, grabbed his books, and put them in a bag. He also unplugged the radio and left the room that had been his home for the last six months.

The next morning, Clara entered the room with two IV bottles. She left them on the table and opened the curtains, whistling. Then, with unusual care, she placed the two bottles on the stand, and said sweetly to the doctor, "Thanks, Doc, I knew you were coming back. Now I don't have to worry: now my Ana's got someone to keep her company."

Triumphant, the old lady walked towards the door. At the threshold she turned her head to look at the two inanimate bodies that listened attentively to the drops fall, like strange music from other worlds.

Wolves

JOSÉ LUIS ZÁRATE

Translated by BERNARDO FERNÁNDEZ
and CHRIS N. BROWN

ॐ

THE WOLVES CAME at twilight,
melted into the shadows. At first we thought they were mist
coming down from the mountains—it was impossible to think
that there were millions of white bodies, thousands of creatures
sliding down the snow. Their voices convinced us it was them,
their long, sad howls, the occasional growling and fights among
them. We've never seen such a herd. It's impossible to gather one
on these lands. The wolves we know around here are solitary,
ferocious animals, always stealthy. We've never seen them trot
into a village. They don't run away from men out of fear; their

temperament demands that they always hide—all carnivores are furtive. Once in a while they steal a sheep, a deer, some child left in the woods that surrounds us.

They are always fleeting, small paces pursuing us in our nightmares. No one has seen them for a long time. All the encounters are fortuitous, almost ethereal. The man or the wolf flees immediately. There's something terrible about staring at the beast, at its deadly eyes, its wild fur, its great strength. Only the victims get to see the wolf in all its magnificence, not casual observers. One senses it's part of a timeless ritual: the ultimate encounter. The voluptuousness of death, of blood spilled on the snow, of flesh offered without resistance to longing fangs.

No one has ever seen how the wolf kills. We imagine a terrible and satisfying ceremony for the beast. At night they cry out their nostalgia for the sweet moments of death.

Wolves are part of nature, brothers of the the blizzards without end, kin to the high-pitched winds. It's the wolves who know which tree is going to fall, the place where the ice across the lake is going to crack, how we will lose our crops. They walk with the certainty that comes with hunger. We do not hate them. We cannot hate that which is part of the cycle of all things. We are just wary of them, keeping our edge.

No one has ever killed a wolf, because to try to do so is as pointless as trying to hold back the snow.

The wolves don't hate us, either—that would make it too easy to kill them. How would we catch them when we are hiding in our houses behind fragile windows?

And now they are coming, a blizzard of wolves, thousands, millions, coming down from the mountains.

What has happened to the villages that found themselves in the path of this bizarre flood?

We don't know. The river of wolves has isolated us from the world. We can see its unending advance, but not its end. Where do they come from? Where are they going? What will become of us?

We have fortified ourselves as best as we can, reinforcing the doors, boarding up the windows, storing enough grain to survive a few days. We have prayed without answer.

We wait.

First the steps, like a steady rain, then the sense of their advance, the fur of the multitude rubbing against our walls, the oppressive odor of their breath.

They are not trying to tear down our houses. They are not fighting to rip our flesh. They trot, just passing by, one, two, three, dozens, hundreds, thousands. We are in the middle of a living current, occasionally interrupted by a small fight—no more.

The river flows without end.

We have opened the windows and not a single wolf has leapt for our throats. They pass by. Their march is not forced. They don't appear to be fleeing.

They walk as if it were natural for millions of wolves to walk among humans.

Days go by and the rhythm does not lessen. The flow is unending. At night we listen to their footsteps. Their smell has impregnated everything. Sometimes we find ourselves growling at each other, drawn into their march. Where are they going? What is waiting for them at their destination?

After dark we come out to observe them, envying their

strength, their determination, feeling ourselves part of the current.

We dream of fresh blood, of the endless woods that belong to us, of seeing the world through bestial eyes.

The air pulses with an immense power. Nothing will hold back the sea of wolves.

This morning I looked at myself in the mirror and didn't recognize myself. Maybe I was dreaming. Or not. The neighbors' doors are open and I have seen more wolves joining the flood. Is that why it is infinite? Because everything it touches, everything it attracts, everything it sees turns into a wolf?

I have not seen any other animals in the woods. Nothing living other than the wolves.

I stare at the moon over our heads, brilliant and obscene. I want to howl at it, rip its luminous flesh. I want to join the pack.

I can barely open the door. My hands no longer exist. I smell the scent that attracts me. Blood on the other side of the world, an ocean heated with red waters.

I stare at the moon.

Since the flood of the wolves began, the full moon hasn't left.

When I howl my love for her, I understand why.

The Infamous Juan Manuel

BRUNO ESTAÑOL

Translated by ANISIA RODRÍGUEZ

For Leonardo Nierman

༄

I AM THE INFAMOUS Juan Manuel, and I reside in Hell. There is no place I would rather be. Soon enough I shall tell you why. For now suffice it to say that I spent my earthly life in search of treasure. I always knew that is what I wanted to do. In my childhood I learned all I could about pirates and the great treasures of the globe. The treasure of Montezuma that Cortez abandoned in Tenochtitlán on "The Sad Night" was the one that most consumed my imagination, though there were many others. As I aged I purchased scores of maps—apocryphal and authentic, ragged and yellow, worn by innumerable fingers throughout the centuries; maps with sea sand that testified to their origins, coded maps, maps that were meant to be seen only if backlit, maps that had been first sold years ago in antique shops in Cairo and London.

I dug in the countryside and in the cemeteries, in the hills and in the fields of wheat, corn, and rice. I destroyed the walls of my home. I explored deep wells and exhausted the beaches where pirates had supposedly left treasure in the form of doubloons, ingots and jewels incrusted in relics, utensils and amulets. I forgot about women, about children, about siblings and parents, about parties, books, and friends. I experienced poverty and hunger. I imagined myself sitting in my bedroom, counting Spanish doubloons and French Gold Louis carefully stacked on my table, my breast filled with inexhaustible happiness. The years passed, but I had yet to find the fabled gold. As I saw my death quickly approaching, I set out for cemeteries, prairies, and forests. I invoked the devil under the full moon to assist me in my search, but he would not deign to appear nor provide me with the slightest clue. I realized that the devil didn't exist then, and I plunged into a deep melancholy. I realized that I had wasted my life, my health, and my money.

One night, attempting to amuse myself, I went to the theater. I slept intermittently throughout the performance. As I observed the actors moving about like puppets, my thoughts continued to center on treasure. There sat a man behind me in the shadows, and my peripheral vision encompassed his luxurious attire and the monocle over his left eye. "It's a boring play," he whispered softly in my ear, "the actors aren't searching for treasure or making pacts with the devil, which would be better suited to your taste." During the following act, he placed two large manila envelopes on my lap, and my eyes instinctively perused them.

They were labeled with gothic letters: the first reading, "How to find the treasure," and the second, "What to do after finding the treasure: Important! Open immediately after finding it, by no means before." The letters were clear and visible despite the theatre's dim light. I don't know why the words *immediately* and *before* sounded urgently in my mind. I turned my head to address him, but his seat was empty. Only seconds before, the gentleman had been there. I left the theatre in haste, wishing to catch him up but not finding him; so I hurried home to open the first envelope.

It crossed my mind that someone might be playing a joke on me, for it was well known that I was obsessed with treasure. Nevertheless, by candlelight I opened the first envelope. I felt my heart tremble. The letters danced in front of my eyes: "Dig one meter below your bed" is all it said. I hardly slept that night. Early the next day, I was ready with a pick, shovel, pails, and buckets, that latter for the purpose of containing the dirt and rubble. The cement floor was as hard as stone, and it was difficult to break it with the pick. Moreover, I was afraid that the noise would be heard in the street and attract unwanted attention. I excavated for more than fifteen hours. Finally, what I had hoped for! The pick struck something metal. It was a square, rusted, iron box about a half-meter wide and a quarter-meter tall. It was extremely heavy, and with difficulty I carried it to the kitchen table. It had a small padlock on it, which I broke with a chisel, and then I removed the rust from around the edges. When I opened the box, the carefully piled coins came into view. One by one I took them out and placed them in stacks of ten. When I had finished arranging them on the table, the first rays of dawn illuminated them. Never in my life had I been happier than at that moment. I believed that occasion was worth all the suffering and sacrifice I had experienced during the course of my lifetime. If only I might preserve this moment forever, I thought.

On the corner of the table I noticed the second envelope, but I gazed upon it with disinterest. All that I had yearned for I had already obtained, and what I intended to do with the treasure was no one's business but my own. All the same, considering the truth that the first envelope contained about my only mission here on earth, I gathered that the second one might reveal further secrets, equaling or surpassing the marvels of the first.

Perhaps there was more treasure to be found! I broke the envelope's seal. The note within said: "Read these words and fall dead upon the table." Dead indeed! All happened according to the writing. On the other side I was informed that if I choose Hell I could eternally relive the moment in which I first observed those gold coins shining brightly at daybreak. My other option was a tranquil life in Heaven, where I could forget that juncture in my life and be cured of my obsession forever. I was convinced that no cure could equal the thrill of the moment my eyes first beheld the treasure in its full splendor. I made my choice, therefore, without the slightest regard for the consequences—and this is the story of how I, of my own volition, made Hell my abode.

COPYRIGHTS

ABOUT THE AUTHORS

漢

AGUSTÍN CADENA (Ixmiquilpan, 1963) is a novelist, short story writer, essayist, poet, and translator, and a university professor of literature. He has published over twenty books in many literary genres and has collaborated on more than fifty publications in various countries. His work has been recognized with many awards. Some of his work has been anthologized in Mexico, Spain, Argentina, USA, and Italy, and translated into English, Italian, and Hungarian.

ALBERTO CHIMAL (Toluca, 1970) is a writer and professor of creative writing. He is the author of the critically lauded novel *Los esclavos* (*The Slaves,* 2009) and sixteen short story collections, including *Grey* (*Flock,* 2006), *Cinco aventuras de Horacio Kustos* (*Five Adventures of Horatio Kustos,* 2008), *La ciudad imaginada y otras historias* (*The Imaginary City and Other Stories,* 2009), and *83 novelas* (*83 Novels,* 2011). He has also written a collection of essays, a translation of Edgar Allan Poe's *Politian* (*Poliziano,* 2010), two plays produced in the late 1990s, the anthology *Viajes celestes* (*Celestial Journeys,* 2006) and a comic: *Horacio en las ciudades* (*Horatio in the Cities,* 2004), illustrated by Ricardo "Micro" Garcia. Mexican critics have cited his work as departing from common themes in contemporary Mexican literature to a territory closer to European and Latin American fantastic literature, merging everyday life with the extraordinary and mythical.

AMPARO DÁVILA (Pinos, Zacatecas, 1928) is a poet and short-story writer. She has published the poetry collections *Salmos bajo la luna* (1950) and *Meditación a la orilla del sueño y Perfil de soledades* (1954). Her fiction works include *Tiempo destrozado* (1959), *Música concreta* (1964), and *Árboles petrificados* (1977), which received the Xavier Villaurrutia Prize.

AMÉLIE OLAIZ (León) is a writer and professor at Universidad Iberoamericana (UIA) and Universidad Intercontinental in Mexico City, where she has lived since childhood.

She studied Graphic Design at UIA and holds a Master's degree in Industrial Design and a Diploma in Creativity from the UIA. In 1996 she started studying Buddhist philosophy. Her literary works have appeared in *Piedras de Luna* (*Moon Stones,* 2005, republished in Spain in 2007) and *Aquí está tu cielo* (*Here Is Your Sky,* 2007), and in the anthologies *Ficticia's Citizens* (2003), *Prohibido fumar* (*No Smoking*, 2008), Infidelidades.con (*Infidelities.with*, 2008), *Antología mínima del orgasmo* (*Minimal Orgasm Anthology*, 2009), and *Vampiros mundanos y transmundanos* (*Mundane and Transmundane Vampires*, 2011). Her work has also appeared in the newspapers *La Jornada*, *El Financiero*, and *Reforma*, the journal *Castálida*, and in various Chilean textbooks. A participant in several writers workshops, she won three first-place prizes in contests organized by the Ficiticia's Matina workshop.

ANA CLAVEL (Mexico City, 1961) is a novelist, short-story writer, and essayist. Her novel *Los deseos y su sombra* (*Desire and Its Shadow*, 2006) was a finalist for the International Alfaguara Prize. Her novel *Cuerpo náufrago* (Alfaguara 2005; *Shipwrecked Body*, Aliform 2008) became Cuerpo náufrago/ ready-made multimedia para bucear en la identidad y el deseo (a performance, photo exhibition, installation, and website). *Las Violetas son flores del deseo* (Alfaguara 2007) won the Radio France International Short Novel Juan Rulfo Prize and was the origin point of a multimedia project that included a sex doll exhibition, installation, performance, and website. Her most recent novel is *El dibujante de sombras* (Alfaguara 2009).

ANA GLORIA ÁLVAREZ PEDRAJO was born in her beloved Mexico on the 17th of December. Since then she writes: "I liked to listen to all kinds of tales, especially ghost stories. We Mexicans keep a tight relationship with our dead friends and family; we take food for them to the cemetery, decorate their tombs with lots of flowers, we sing and we talk to them daily. I remember the distress caused by the falling soil on my grandmother's coffin. She always had been energetic and of cheerful temperament. My

mind, then a child's mind, couldn't understand how that phenomenon, the one called "death" by the adults, could keep her
from her sad fate. My father, aware of this, explained to me that
this life is not the real one; that the happiness we all desperately
seek is only possible in the eternity with God. I believe the re-
currence of unearthly and mystic topics in my work is caused by
this first impression. I can say that the spirits and I are friends,
we understand each other. Neither they nor I belong to this
world; them for their condition, I by my inability to adapt and
because my soul longs and sensed the beauty of the intangible
and immaterial universe."

BEATRIZ ESCALANTE is the author of novels, short stories,
essays, and academic textbooks. Her publications include *Los
pegasos de la memoria, Júrame que te casaste virgen,* and *El marido
perfecto.* She lives in Mexico City.

BERNARDO FERNÁNDEZ (Mexico City, 1972), aka **Bef**, is a
novelist, comic-book artist, and graphic designer. He has published the novels *Tiempo de alacranes* (*Scorpions Season*, 2005), *Gel
azul* (*Blue Gel*, 2006), *Ladrón de sueños* (*The Dream Thief*, 2008)
and *Ojos de lagarto* (*Snake Eyes*, 2009); the short-story collections
¡¡Bzzzzzzt!! Ciudad interfase (*¡¡Bzzzzzzt!! Interface City*, 1998) and
El llanto de los niños muertos (*The Crying of the Dead Children*,
2008); the children's books *Error de programación* (*Software Error*,
1997), *Cuento de hadas para conejos* (*Fairy Tales for Bunnies*, 2007),
Groar and *Soy el robot* (*I Am the Robot*, 2010); short comic-book
stories *Pulpo cómics* (*Octopus Comics*, 2004), *Monorama* (2007), and
Monorama 2 (2009) and the graphic novels *Perros Muertos* (Dead
Dogs, 2006), *Espiral* (*Spiral*, 2010) and *La Calavera de Cristal* (*The
Crystal Skull*, 2011). Called by some one of the best young Mexican

writers of our times, he has won several prizes, including the Mexican national novel prize Otra Vuelta de Tuerca, the Spanish Memorial Silverio Cañada prize for best first crime novel, and the Ignotus prize of the Spanish Association of Fantasy, Science Fiction and Horror. His latest novel, *Hielo Negro* (*Black Ice*), a thriller about the narco culture, received the 2011 Grijalbo Novel Award. He is currently working on *Uncle Bill*, a graphic novel about the American writer William Burroughs and his time in Mexico.

BRUNO ESTAÑOL was born in a little port of the Gulf of Mexico, Frontera Tabasco, Mexico. He writes mainly short novels and stories as well as essays. He is a neurologist and professor of clinical neurophysiology at the National University of Mexico.

CARMEN RIOJA (Monterrey, 1975) is a Mexican writer and artist. She has participated in several literary workshops with writers such as María Luisa Puga, Guillermo Samperio, Juan Villorio, Antonio Vilanova, and Jorge Hernández among others. Rioja studied Hispanic Letters and has published the short story collection *La Muerte Niña* (El Hechicero Books), which includes the story "La Casa de Chayo" ("Chayo's House") adapted into an IMCINE award-winning short film by Guissepe Solano. Carmen has also published poetry in magazines and periodicals; the poem *Vuelo Aerostático sobre Teotihuacán* (*Air Balloon Flight over Teotihuacán*) is included in the anthology *Corazón Prestado: El Mundo Precolombino en la Poesía de los Siglos XIX y XX* (*Borrowed Heart: The Pre-Columbian World in the Poetry of the 19th & 20th Centuries*). Her work has appeared in the newspaper *El Corregidor* of Querétaro, and she served as co-producer and host of the literary critique radio show *Sancho Panza de Cabeza*. Currently, she writes her blog *Hojas al Rio* (Leaves on the River). She is also a conservation artist specializing in colonial and archaeological collections, and works in cultural and art promotion. Her involvement in plastic arts includes several painting techniques and sculpture.

CLAUDIA GUILLÉN (Mexico City, 1963) is a writer of fiction and essays. She won the Young Creators scholarship from FONCA in the short-story category and from the same institution the Abroad Residencies scholarship in Salzburg, Austria. Her short story "La cita" won the XXXV Latin-American Edmundo Valadés Short Story award. She writes for *Revista de la Universidad de México* and *Diario Milenio*. Her literary work has appeared in *La insospechada María y otras mujeres* (*The Unexpected Mary and Other Womena*) and *Los otros* (*The Others*), and the anthologies *Un hombre a la medida* (*A Man to the Extent*, which she also edited), *Con licencia para escribir* (*Licensed to Write*), *Cuentos Violentos* (*Violent Stories*), *Prohibido fumar* (*No Smoking*), *Atrapados en la escuela* (*Trapped in School*) and *Sólo cuento* (*Only Story*). Some of her work has also been translated to English and French.

DONAJÍ OLMEDO was born in Distrito Federal, México, 1964. She is a graduate of Universidad Nacional Autónoma de México and has a cardiology postgraduate degree from the Instituto Mexicano del Seguro Social. She has taken part in many literary workshops, mainly short story and microfiction, at Casa Refugio Citlaltépec at the Fundación Cultural Samperio, A.C. Her literary work has been concentrated mainly on short stories and short novel. She has a blog and a website, "Casa de Ateh," where she publishes her own literature and other Mexican authors.

EDMÉE PARDO (Mexico City, 1965) is the author of many novels and collections, including *The Blue Voice* and *Sickness is*

Written With a C. She is a founding member of the independent publishing house Brujas and founding partner of Amati (a literature workshop space). She is an experienced journalist and is a commentator on the "Abra Palabra" program. She teaches at Amati and La Casa Universitaria del Libro. Her website is edmeepardo.com.

ESTHER M. GARCIA (Cd. Juárez, 1987) is a writer, journalist, and photographer. She holds a degree in Spanish Literature from the Autonomous University of Coahuila. She received the National Short Story Prize Criaturas de la noche in 2008, and published the poetry collection *La Doncella Negra* (2010), and the short-story collection *Las Tijeras de Átropos* (2011). Other stories have been anthologized in *Los Nuevos Románticos.* Her journalistic work has appeared in newspapers and magazines including *Espacio 4, Palabra, Vanguardia, La i Saltillo, Día Siete, Plaza Ludens, Lóbulo temporal, palabrasmalditas.net* and *Pirocromo.*

GABRIELA DAMIÁN MIRAVETE (Mexico City, 1979) is a writer, journalist, editor, and lecturer. She has a masters in Communication from the Universidad Autónoma de Barcelona and degrees in creative writing from the SOGEM Escuela de Escritores and in the literature of the fantastic from the Universidad del Claustro de Sor Juana. She received the Story Prize from the Feria Internacional del Libro Infantil y Juvenil (FILIJ) for *La Tradición de Judas* (illustrated by Cecilia Varela) and grant from the Fondo Nacional para la Cultura y las Artes de México, with the support of which she wrote *Pequeños naipes de opalo,* a volume of fantastic stories themed around the seasons, which includes "Future Nereid." Each week she recommends strange books—like this one—on the radio program Ecléctico, and she participates in the feminist broadcast Nuestra habitación both on Código DF radio and online. She lives with three cats, waiting patiently for the day when she can replace them with a dragon. Her blog lives on at: naipesdeopalo.blogsome.com

GERARDO SIFUENTES (Tampico, 1974) is a journalist and author of short stories. He was co-founder of the pioneer Spanish-language cyberpunk zine *Fractal*. His work has been collected twice, in *Perro de Luz* (*Light Dog*, 1999) and *Pilotos Infernales* (*Infernal Pilots*, 2002), and appeared in various magazines and anthologies, earning the Kalpa Prize for best short story published in Mexico and the 2002 Vid International Fantasy and Science Fiction Award for the best collection. He is currently editorial coordinator of *Muy Interesante* (*Very Interesting*), a popular science and history magazine.

GUILLERMO SAMPERIO (Mexico City, 1948). He has written more than twenty books, including short stories, novels, essays, children's literature, and poetry. His most recent books are: *Cuentos Reunidos* (Alfaguara, Mexico); *Cómo se escribe un cuento 500 Tips para nuevos cuentistas del siglo XXI* (Berenice, Spain); *La guerra oculta*, cuentos, (Lectorum, México). His work has been translated into multiple languages. He is director of the Despacho de Ingeniería Cultural, S.C., presidente de la Fundación Cultural Samperio, A.C., newspaper columnist and contributor to the financial magazine *Siempre!*, *Día Siete*, *La Jornada Semanal y Laberinto* (Milenio), among others. His most recent books are *Marcos, el enmascarado de estambre*, (biografía no autorizada y novelada), (Editorial Lectorum, Mexico), and an anthology of short stories, prose poetry, and a novel titled *Maravillas malabares* (Editorial Cátedra, Spain). He lives in Mexico City.

HERNÁN LARA ZAVALA is a short-story writer, novelist, and essayist. Although he was born in Mexico City, his family comes from Yucatan, where many of his stories are set. He is the author of a novel, *Península Península*, which was awarded the Real Academia Española Award, and a number of short-story collections. He lives in México City, where he teaches at the University of Mexico.

HORACIO SENTÍES MADRID was born in Mexico City in 1970. Dr. Senties is an Honorary Fellow in Internal Medicine at the Cleveland Clinic Foundation and a Headache Fellow at the Headache Clinic in Houston, Texas. He has given 146 lectures and has published 117 articles, book chapters, and abstracts in medical books and journals, and is a member of the editorial committee of multiple medical journals. Dr. Sentíes is Neurology professor (Panamericana University and Superior Studies Technological Institute of Monterrey), Neurophysiology professor (postgraduate course, UNAM). He was the Secretary of the Mexican Academy of Neurology and is the coordinator of Adults Latinoamerican Commission of the International League Against Epilepsy and Vicepresident of Epilepsy Mexican Chapter. He has published cultural essays (e.g., "The Enigma of Synesthesia" in *Letras Libres*) and fiction. He is also a piano composer.

ILIANA ESTAÑOL (Mexico City, 1978) began taking pictures at the age of eleven with an old Canon camera that her father gave her. At about the same age, she started writing poetry and short stories. It didn't take long until she started making long photography series. Telling stories with still images became her passion. But the happiness didn't last, she soon realized that she wanted those images to move. She studied film direction and screenwriting in Cuba, Berlin, and Zurich. Since 1999 she has written and directed several movies and has continued to write short stories. She has worked in Burkina Faso, Korea, Austria, Italy, Switzerland, Germany, Brasil, Cuba and of course Mexico.

JESÚS RAMÍREZ BERMÚDEZ (Mexico City, 1973) studied medicine, psychiatry, and neuropsychiatry, and received a master's and doctorate in Medical Sciences at the Universidad Nacional Autonoma de Mexico (UNAM). He is Chief of the Neuropsychiatry Unit of the National Institute of Neurology and Neurosurgery. He has received national and international awards for his work as a researcher. His stories and essays have been published in *Dosfilos, Inland, The Day Weekly,* and *The Tempest.* In 2006 he published the novel *Confabulation,* chosen by the newspapers *Reforma, Milenio,* and *Proceso,* as among the best of the year. In 2007 he received the "Young Creators" grant from the National Fund for Culture and the Arts for his book of essays, *A Short Clinical Dictionary of the Soul.*

JOSÉ LUIS ZÁRATE (Puebla, 1966) is one of the best-known contemporary Mexican authors of science fiction, as well as having written works outside the genre. His best-known novels include *Xanto, noveluche libre* (*Santo,* 1994), *La ruta del hielo y sal* (*The Road of Ice and Salt,* 1998), and *Del cielo oscuro y del abismo* (*The Dark Sky and the Abyss,* 2001), together forming the trilogy *The Phases of Myth* in which the popular culture figures Dracula, Superman, and the Mexican masked wrestler El Santo are seen from the perspective of residents of their fictional worlds. His other works include the novel *Ventana 654 ¿Cuánto Falta para el Futuro?* (*Window 654: How Far to the Future?,* 2004), the short-story collections *El viajero* (*The Traveler,* 1987), *Permanencia Voluntaria*

(*Volunteer Retention*, 1990), *Magia* (*Magic*, 1994), *Las razas ocultas* (*The Hidden Races*, 1999), *Hyperia* (1999), and *Quitzá y otros sitios* (*Quitzá and Other Sites*, 2002), and the essay collection *En el principio fue el sangre* (*In the Beginning was the Blood*, 2004). A founder of the Mexican Science Fiction Association, his works have won various national and international awards.

KAREN CHACEK (Mexico City, a Saturday in 1972) is an inhabitant of parallel worlds and a storyteller. She spent her childhood surrounded by comics, TV series, and fables. As a teenager, she discovered novels, science fiction, music videos, and film. Her fascination with the visual language drove her to study film. Today she's a writer and a screenwriter. She has published the short-story collection *Parallel Days* (2006) and the children's books *An Unexpected Pet* (2007) and *Nina Complot* (2009). Her short fiction has also appeared in various anthologies of chronicle, horror, science fiction, and children's stories. She has also worked as a video post producer and written for science, technology, and travel magazines. In 2001 she was invited to participate in the Mexico-Barcelona Sundance Institute workshop. She is passionate about her long walks in public parks, loves cloudy days, insects, cats, underground passages, and dystopias.

LEO MENDOZA (Oaxaca, 1958) has published four short-story collections, has edited a few anthologies, and his writing has been included and even translated in others. He has practiced many kinds of cultural journalism and years ago sold kitchen appliances. As a screenwriter he has written many TV programs and two movies: *Teo's Journey* (2008), based on his screenplay, and *Hidalgo/Molière*, ultimately titled *Hidalgo: The Untold Story* (2009). Mendoza has won several awards such as the San Luis Potosí

National Short Story prize and the Benemérito de América in Oaxaca. He won the National Culture and Arts Fund scholarship and in 2006 became a member of the National Creators System. In recent years he has mainly worked as a screenwriter, but also managed to write a collaborative novel about Pre-hispanic Mexico. Currently Mendoza's main ambitions include reading, eating, watching movies, traveling and having sufficient time to write. In spite of his advancing age he is often astonished, although he now accepts the fact that he will never play center forward on his Atlante soccer team.

LILIANA V. BLUM (Mexico) is not one of those women who refuse to reveal their date of birth; she just likes coincidences. So that she was born the same year that Heinrich Böll's *The Lost Honor of Katharina Blum* was published, is a great one. She is a ginger gal who suffered through her Mexican childhood of pinch-the-redhead-in-the-arm-for-luck. Now she only suffers the sun. She was born in Durango (famous for its scorpions, revolutionaries, and narcos) and currently lives in Tampico, Tamaulipas (famous for its crabs and narco-related violence). Despite the eight-legged creatures, the daily bread of bullets and mutilated bodies, and being the mother of a boy, a girl, a beagle, and a guinea pig, she has managed to write five short-story collections; one of them, *The Curse of Eve and Other Stories* (Host Publications, 2007) was translated into English. Her work has been published in literary magazines in the US, Mexico, England, and Poland. One of her books will be reprinted for a reading campaign in Mexico City, to give away for free in the subway. She is currently working on her first novel.

LUCÍA ABDÓ'S story in Spanish is "Segunda calle de

Pachuca"—the street she lives on in México City, in the Condesa
neighborhood, one of the most representative places of the syn-
cretism of Mexican identity.

MARÍA ISABEL AGUIRRE was born in Mexico City. She holds
a B.A. in Spanish literature and reports that she mostly writes
poetry but occasionally also writes fiction.

MAURICIO MONTIEL FIGUEIRAS (Guadalajara, 1968) is a fic-
tion writer, essayist, poet, and translator. He is the author of the
short-story collections *Donde la piel es un tibio silencio* (*Where the
Skin is a Silent Warmth*, 1992), *Páginas para una siesta húmeda* (*Pages
for a Wet Siesta*, 1992), *Insomnios del otro lado* (*Insomnia on the Other
Side*, 1994), *La penumbra inconveniente* (*Inconvenient Darkness*, 2001),
La piel insomne (*The Sleepless Skin*, 2002), and *Los animales invisibles*
(*The Invisible Animals*, 2009), the poetry collections *Mirando cómo
arde la amarga ciudad* (*Watching the Bitter City Burn*, 1994) and
Oscuras palabras para escuchar a Satie (*Dark Words for Listening to
Satie*, 1995), and the essay collection *Terra Cognita* (2007). He
received the Edmundo Valadés Latin American Short Story
Prize in 2000 and the Elías Nandino Poetry Prize in 1993. He has
worked as editor and columnist for various journals and cultural
supplements, including *Letras Libres*, *Día Siete*, and *El Universal*,
and as Director of Publishing of the National Museum of Art in
Mexico City. He was a fellow of the National Endowment for the
Arts and Culture and of the Rockefeller Foundation, fulfilling a
residency at the Bellagio Study and Conference Center in 2008.

MÓNICA LAVÍN (Mexico City, 1955) has published seven short-
story books and seven novels. She won the 1997 Gilberto Owen
National Award for her short-story collection *Ruby Tuesday no ha*

muerto (*Ruby Tuesday is not Dead*); the 2001 Narrativa de Colima for the best book of the year for *Café cortado* (*Cut Coffee*), and the 2010 Premio Iberoamericano de Novela Elena Poniatowska for her novel about Sor Juana, *Yo, la peor* (*Me, The Worst,* which has been reprinted several times). She is a professor at the Creative Writing Department at the Autonomous University of Mexico City; writes for the newspaper *El Universal,* and recommends books on radio. Her short stories have been translated to English, French, and Italian and are included in national and international anthologies. She lives in Mexico City and is a member of the Sistema Nacional de Creadores.

ÓSCAR DE LA BORBOLLA (Mexico City, 1949) is an essayist, novelist, and poet. He received his Ph.D. from the Universidad Complutense de Madrid. His work has been translated into English, French, and Serbo-Croatian.

PEPE ROJO (Chilpancingo, 1968) has published four books and more than 200 short stories, essays, and articles dealing with fiction, media, and contemporary culture, including the 2009 collection *Interrupciones* (*Interruptions*). He teaches in the Taller (e) Media program at the Autonomous University of Baja California (UABC) in Tijuana. With Deyanira Torres and Bernardo Fernández, he co-founded Pellejo/Molleja, an indie publishing firm, where he edited *Sub* (sub-genre literature), *Número X* (media culture) and *Pulpo Comics* (a Mexican-sf comics anthology). With Torres, he co-produced and co-directed a series of interventions, "You Don't Exist," as well as the video installation series "Psicopanoramas". He produced two interactive stories (*Masq* and *Club Ciel*) for *Alteraction,* and published two collections of Minibúks (*Mexican SF* and *Counter-versions*) at UABC, as well as the graphic intervention "Philosophical Dictionary of Tijuana." In April and May 2011 he produced a series of sf-based interventions and lectures at the Tijuana-San Ysidro border crossing, "You Can See the Future from Here," with students from UABC, as well as U.S. science fiction writers including Bruce Sterling and Chris N. Brown. He lives in strange Tijuana with his strange Lacanian psychoanalyst wife, Deyanira Torres, and two strange kids (and by *strange,* he of course means "lovely in an endearing and unusual kind of way").

QUETA NAVAGÓMEZ was born in Bellavista, Nayarit, in western Mexico. She holds a Bachelor Degree in Physical Education, a Diploma in Script Writing and Literary Creation from the General Society of Mexican Writers, and a Seminary in Literary Creation from the National Autonomous University of Mexico (UNAM). She represented her country at track and field competitions at the Central American games. She has won several literary awards for her short fiction, poetry, and literary novels (*Marie Claire Magazine's Writing Contest 1995,* National Poetry Award "Ali Chumacero," 2003-2004, *National Novel Award "Jose Ruben Romero," INBA, 2008*). Her stories, poetry and novels have been published in journals and anthologies in the U.S.A., Mexico, Argentina, Spain, Venezuela, Chile, and Peru. She lives in Mexico City, where she participates actively in regional and national cultural activities.

RENÉ ROQUET (Mexico City, 1969) has worked as a gardener, painter, in a parts store, renovator, and bank teller. He has published reviews, literary criticism, and short stories in many newspapers and magazines and in three anthologies.

YUSSEL DARDÓN (Puebla, 1982) is author of *Maquetas del Universo* (*Models of the Universe*) and *Fractatus Vitae*. His first book of short stories was described as "shows the brightness of a serious and nuanced work." He has published in national and international journals and was anthologized in the Spring 2010 number dedicated to "Obsession" from the *Rio Grande Review*, a bilingual publication of the University of Houston. He was selected as a Young Artists Fellow of the National Fund for Culture and the Arts for 2010-11.

ABOUT THE EDITORS

Born in Boston and raised in San Antonio, **EDUARDO JIMÉNEZ MAYO** holds an undergraduate degree from Harvard University in Hispanic literature and a doctoral degree in the humanities from a Catholic university in Madrid. He has taught undergraduate literature courses at the University of Texas in San Antonio and recently obtained a doctorate in jurisprudence from Cornell Law School. He has published translations of books by contemporary Mexican authors Bruno Estañol, Rafael Pérez Gay, and José María Pérez Gay. In recent years, he has also published scholarly studies on the Spanish poet Antonio Machado and the Mexican fiction writer Bruno Estañol. Lately, he has conducted readings and lectures on the subject of literary translation at the invitation of Cornell University, New York University, The New School, and the Juárez Autonomous University of Tabasco.

CHRIS N. BROWN writes fiction and criticism from his home in Austin, Texas. His work has been variously described as "slick, post-Gibsonian, and funny as hell, like Neal Stephenson meets Hunter S. Thompson" (Cory Doctorow), "JG Ballard with a Texas twang" (SF Site), "Borges in a pop culture blender" (Invisible Library), and "like a cross between Mark Leyner and William Gibson" (Boing Boing); he calls it "pulp fiction for smart people." A bibliography with links to work online can be found at www.nakashima-brown.net.

Since 2001, Small Beer Press, an independent publishing house, has published satisfying and surreal novels and short story collections by award-winning writers and exciting talents whose names you may never have heard, but whose work you'll never be able to forget:

Joan Aiken, *The Monkey's Wedding and Other Stories*
Ted Chiang, *Stories of Your Life and Others*
Georges-Olivier Chateaureynaud, *A Life on Paper* (trans. Edward Gauvin)
John Crowley, *The Chemical Wedding**
Alan DeNiro, *Skinny Dipping in the Lake of the Dead*
Hal Duncan, *An A-Z of the Fantastic City**
Carol Emshwiller, *Carmen Dog; The Mount; Report to the Men's Club*
Karen Joy Fowler, *What I Didn't See and Other Stories*
Greer Gilman, *Cloud & Ashes: Three Winter's Tales*
Angélica Gorodischer, *Kalpa Imperial* (trans. Ursula K. Le Guin); *Trafalgar**
(trans. by Amalia Gladheart)
Alasdair Gray, *Old Men in Love: John Tunnock's Posthumous Papers*
Elizabeth Hand, *Errantry: Stories*; Generation Loss; Mortal Love**
Kij Johnson, *At the Mouth of the River of Bees: Stories**
Nancy Kress, *Fountain of Age: Stories**
Kelly Link, *Magic for Beginners; Stranger Things Happen; Trampoline* (Editor)
Karen Lord, *Redemption in Indigo: a novel*
Maureen F. McHugh, *Mothers & Other Monsters, After the Apocalypse*
Naomi Mitchison, *Travel Light*
Benjamin Rosenbaum, *The Ant King and Other Stories*
Geoff Ryman, *The Child Garden; The King's Last Song; Paradise Tales; Was*
Sofia Samatar, *A Stranger in Olondria**
Delia Sherman & Christopher Barzak (Eds.), *Interfictions 2*
Ray Vukcevich, *Meet Me in the Moon Room*
Kate Wilhelm, *Storyteller*
Howard Waldrop, *Howard Who?*

Big Mouth House Titles for Readers of All Ages

Joan Aiken, *The Serial Garden: The Complete Armitage Family Stories*
Holly Black, *The Poison Eaters and Other Stories*
Lydia Millet, *The Fires Beneath the Sea: a novel*
Lydia Millet, *The Shimmers in the Night: a novel**
Delia Sherman, *The Freedom Maze: a novel*

*Forthcoming

Our ebooks are available from our indie press ebooksite:
www.weightlessbooks.com

www.smallbeerpress.com